She looked at him, and in an instant every other thought fled.

David was so close and he looked so good. Krissie had almost believed that she would never feel this yearning again…this yearning to be close to a man, to be held, to be touched.

To know whether the yearning she felt now could erupt into the maelstrom of passion.

"You're so beautiful," he whispered, and kissed her lightly again.

More sizzles, more sparkles ran through her. Had she ever felt this way before? Not quite. Not quite like this or so quickly.

Danger. She didn't know him yet. Not well enough….

Dear Reader,

The idea for this book was born out of my concern for some unsung heroes. We are aware of our combat vets, and the dangers they face. Too often we forget the people *they* depend on: the medics, nurses and doctors who face the same risks, the same horrors.

I cannot praise enough the military medical people I've known, from medics in the field (now *there's* heroism), to those who function in field hospitals that are not always safe from attack. They risk their lives to bring relief and healing. I've never known a medic, a nurse or a doctor who didn't also treat civilian casualties whenever they could.

And then there are the hospital ships. One of our greatest gifts to Indonesia after the tsunami was the presence of a hospital ship. We sent her and her wonderful facilities and staff to help the injured and sick, and many of these medical people ventured ashore, despite warnings that they could be targets of warring factions.

These people bear scars, too. People who have devoted themselves to one of the highest callings: saving human lives. And they venture into places willingly where few of us would choose to go. God bless them all.

Rachel

NEW YORK TIMES BESTSELLING AUTHOR

RACHEL LEE

The Unexpected Hero

Silhouette®

Romantic

SUSPENSE

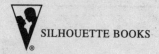 SILHOUETTE BOOKS

Recycling programs
for this product may
not exist in your area.

ISBN-13: 978-0-373-27637-0

THE UNEXPECTED HERO

RACHEL LEE

was hooked on writing by the age of twelve, and practiced her craft as she moved from place to place all over the United States. This *New York Times* bestselling author now resides in Florida and has the joy of writing full-time.

Her bestselling Conard County miniseries (see www.conardcounty.com) has won the hearts of readers worldwide, and it's no wonder, given her own approach to life and love. As she says, "Life is the biggest romantic adventure of all—and if you're open and aware, the most marvelous things are just waiting to be discovered."

To my editor, my agent and the many others
who help bring Conard County to life,
from copy editors to cover artists.

Chapter 1

She thought it was going to be a good evening. Finally.

Kristin Tate, known to family and friends as Krissie, stood at the nurses' station and looked out the window across the corridor at a view of purpling Wyoming mountains to the west as the sun settled for the night. It was, she told herself, good to be home in Conard County.

Six years in the navy followed by eighteen months at the VA hospital in Denver had thoroughly killed any taste she had for the so-called excitement of trauma care. If she lived the rest of her life without ever seeing another human being in that kind of condition, it wouldn't be long enough.

But tonight, her first night on her new job at Conard County's community hospital, it felt good to be in scrubs and facing a patient load of ordinary illnesses, and taking care of people who would recover.

A review of the charts assured her she would face no major difficulties: a kid with a broken leg in traction by himself in a room. An older man with phlebitis receiving anticoagulants. She'd need to check him frequently. A woman with congestive heart failure who seemed to be recovering nicely as her fluid retention diminished. A gastritis that should be ready to go home in the morning, along with a dehydration case and a man with diverticulitis on IV antibiotics.

Straightforward, likely totally uncomplicated. An easy night of checking up on patients who were getting better. God, what a relief that was going to be.

Julie and Nancy, the two licensed practical nurses sharing her shift, were off down the corridor, beginning to usher visitors out for the night. Both LPNs seemed nice, if terribly young, and she wondered if they were new to the area, or if she had somehow just forgotten them. It was possible. They would have still been kids when she left for nursing school, well beneath her radar.

And all these thoughts, she realized as she looked at the mountains, were thoughts designed to distract her from the familiar antiseptic smells that could so easily cause her to regurgitate memories of horrors best forgotten.

The sound of rapid footsteps drew her attention down the hall.

A man bore down on the nurses' station looking a bit like a thundercloud. Dark-haired, dark-eyed, a bit rough around the edges, as if he were too busy to worry about things like haircuts and five o'clock shadow. He wore blue scrubs beneath a white coat. As she watched him approach, she saw her two LPNs glance at each other and dart into separate patient rooms. One of *those,* she thought, somewhere between amusement and impatience.

"Ms. Tate," he said peremptorily.

She stiffened a bit at his tone, and scanned his name plate: Dr. David Marcus. She'd heard a new doctor had started since her last visit home, and this must be him. She forced herself to reply pleasantly, "Yes, doctor?"

"Before we begin, I'd like a few words with you."

Okay, Kristin thought, as she followed him to an empty patient room. One of *those.* Big ego, martinet, wanting everyone to kowtow just so to him. Well, she'd dealt with that kind before. If he was the only thorn on the rose of this new job, she could handle it.

In the patient room, he tossed down a chart he was carrying on the bed and faced her from the far side. His brows lowered, making him appear angry.

"Close the door," he said. No *please* or *thank you.* Forcing her face to remain empty of expression, she gave the door a quick tug. On its pneumatics, it swung slowly closed behind her.

Then, as a result of years of long training in the navy, she assumed the at-ease position: feet spread, hands clasped behind her back. That was the most she would give him.

"I read your jacket," he said.

Kristin stared at him, wondering where the devil this was going? She had ample training and experience as a nurse and excellent recommendations. Did he have something against the navy? "Yes, sir?"

"I know about your experience. I know the conditions you practiced under, because I practiced under similar conditions years ago, with the army."

And this meant?

"Yes, doctor."

"I want to make it very clear that this is a different kind of medicine we practice here."

"That's what I was hoping." She tried to smile, but her dislike for him was rapidly growing. Kind of sad, because he was actually an attractive man. Not that she wanted to be attracted to *any* man right now.

"The thing is, Ms. Tate, on severe emergencies, we stabilize and transport. The cases we have here are uncomplicated. They don't require any extraordinary measures, as a rule, and they don't require any creative treatment. I know what it's like in a field hospital and in a trauma center, and I'm telling you right now, you *will* follow proper protocols at all times, and you will *not* step outside your legal responsibilities as a nurse."

That's when she began to simmer. Really simmer. Part of her wanted to take him on and ask what kind of yahoo he thought she was, what kind of nurse? Instead she kept her voice level. "Nurse practitioner," she corrected.

"Nurse whatever, I don't care. Your experience is all wrong for this kind of hospital, and I want you to be aware of it before you make a decision you have no authority to make. I want you to review protocols to refamiliarize yourself with the *proper* way to practice medicine. Are we clear?"

"Yes, sir!" she said smartly, when what she really wanted to do was crawl across that bed and shake him until his teeth rattled. Who did he think he was? And how dare he make judgments about her when he knew absolutely nothing about her or the way she worked?

"I *will* be watching you," he said sternly. "Now let's go on rounds."

She followed him, feeling like a dog on an extremely tight leash, waiting for a command to sit or roll over. A nurse didn't go on rounds with a doctor, didn't trot after him this way. A nurse was supposed to be treated as a professional who could read a patient's chart and follow the orders on it, not as someone who needed to be instructed on every step in the treatment plan, certainly not in uncomplicated cases like these.

With the patients, however, he was a different man entirely. Trying to swallow her anger with him, she watched as he spoke gently to the boy and to the older patients, showing genuine interest in everything they said as he checked them out and entered information about them on the computer that now held pride of place in each room, having replaced the old paper charts.

In the last room, however, things changed. Mrs. Hester Alexander lay on her bed, asleep. She was recovering from congestive heart failure. Her chart showed she had already lost about thirty pounds of excess water, and her urine outputs were subsiding as the edema vanished. Her heart monitor trace showed a slightly altered lambda wave, sure indicator that a heart attack at some point had caused enough damage to her heart muscle to lead to the arrhythmia which had caused the edema. The lady had been drowning in her own bodily fluids, but now was stabilizing at near normal. The arrhythmia was also being treated.

Dr. Marcus moved quietly, gently palpating the woman's skin to test its sponginess. "That's good," he murmured. "That's excellent. If she's still doing well tomorrow, we may be able to send her home."

"That'll make her happy," Krissie volunteered

quietly. "Earlier she was talking about how tired she is of being here."

For the first time, David Marcus smiled. "She's been complaining about everything since she got here. She especially hates the salt-free diet."

"We talked about that. I made her promise to give it two weeks, and assured her by then she won't miss the salt anymore."

At that he faced her. "She has to stay on this diet forever, not just two weeks."

"I didn't tell her…" Krissie trailed off as Marcus turned away. Her simmer rose a notch closer to boil.

"What's that doll?"

"Doll?" Reluctantly, Krissie stepped closer to look across the bed. On the pillow, partially tucked under the blanket, was an awkwardly sewn doll, made of stuffed hopsacking. The eyes and mouth had been stitched of brightly colored embroidery floss. "The family must have left it."

"It shouldn't be in the bed. We don't know what's in it."

At once Krissie stepped around him and removed it, placing it on the window ledge. She looked at it, feeling unnerved in some way. "It looks like a child did it."

David Marcus came to stand beside her. "Yeah," he said after a moment. "She doesn't have any small children or grandchildren, though."

"Maybe something she made when *she* was a child?"

"Could be." With that, the doctor turned away, as if he were done with the doll. He typed a few things into the computer. "I want to cut her dose of diuretics by half and see how she's doing in the morning. Start that immediately, and keep a close eye."

"Yes, doctor."

"If, for any reason, the change seems to cause the slightest distress, raise the dose immediately and call me."

"Yes, doctor."

Back at the nurses' station, he began to scrawl notes in manila folders he apparently kept for his personal records. Krissie left him to it, walking the floor again to find her LPNs busying themselves tightening beds and talking to patients…in short, taking the low profile and staying out of the way.

Which told her a *lot* about Dr. David Marcus. The only question remaining was *why* he was such a pain. Was he an egotist? A perfectionist? Or was there something more?

And here she'd been thinking that she'd come home to calm and peace and a nursing job that wouldn't wake her with nightmares. Boy, her dad was going to have a laugh at this. The former sheriff had warned her just last week when she'd finally come home for good, "Krissie, baby, the harder you look for peace, the more elusive it gets."

Yup, he was going to have a major laugh at her expense.

David Marcus was still at the nurses' station when she returned. She considered walking past and finding another place to busy herself, then decided that avoidance wasn't going to solve the problem or make her situation with him any easier. Best to just act like nothing had happened.

She settled into the chair at the station, checking all the monitors and finding everything green. Even Mrs. Alexander appeared to be still soundly asleep. The poor dear probably needed to catch up on a lot of rest after what she had been through.

Dr. Marcus cleared his throat. Krissie reluctantly looked his way.

His expression revealed little, but he said, "I guess I should explain."

Krissie remained silent. She wasn't going to give this man an inch unless she had to. He wasn't the only one allowed to get angry.

"Until about three years ago, I was in the army. Iraq mainly."

The light in Krissie's brain began to come on.

He looked down at the folders in front of him. "Ms. Tate, I know what we had to do in those field hospitals. Medicine gets *invented* under those conditions. And before medical school, I was a medic. I…just know that kind of experience can affect how we practice in the civilian world. Sometimes we do things that could cost us our licenses under normal conditions."

At that Krissie gave him a nod. No more, just a nod. He was looking at her now, his dark eyes steady.

"The transition can be difficult. I know from personal experience. I should have handled this better, but sometimes…" He left the sentence dangling.

She understood a lot of the freight he was referring to, stuff that just stayed with you like coal dust in a rail car. She decided to meet him halfway.

Rising, she held out her hand. "Let's start again," she said. "Hi, I'm Krissie Tate. Nice to meet you, doctor."

"Just call me David," he said with a crooked smile, and shook her hand.

"Krissie," she agreed. She even managed a smile.

"Part of the reason I came home was because I don't want to have to invent medicine anymore."

He nodded and finally, finally, his face fully relaxed into a pleasant, even attractive, smile. "It can still come up to bite you. Take it from me."

And there it was. He had been reacting to his own difficult transition and to his expectation she would have the same problem, perhaps even make the same mistakes. And he might be right, she admitted honestly. While time with the VA had helped ease her back, she hadn't come back all the way, because VA hospitals were woefully underfunded and under-staffed. She'd had to "invent medicine" there sometimes, too.

"Okay," she said. "I'll take the warning the way it was meant, not the way it was given."

At that, a chuckle escaped him. "Fair enough," he agreed. "I *was* heavy-handed about it, as if you'd already done something wrong."

"I haven't had time to mess up yet," she said on a humorous note.

"And you probably won't. It's just that I know how long it takes to come back from all that adrenaline."

"Meaning?"

"You walk in, you smell the antiseptics, the other things that you identify as hospital, and after years of experience in wartime conditions, the adrenaline auto-matically kicks in. We're like Pavlovian dogs in that respect. We go up the instant the smells hit our noses."

She nodded slowly. "I guess you're right. But I spent the last year and a half at the VA in Denver."

"Still stressful, even if it's not as bad. Anyway, you and I learned trauma medicine under the worst imaginable circumstances. It's not something you can shuck easily like worn-out clothes."

"No, it's not," she admitted. "I felt it when I first walked in here tonight. I had to remind myself this is different."

"Exactly. Anyway, I guess I was harsher and more critical than I needed to be by far."

She pursed her lips. "You *might* say that."

He flashed another smile, quickly. "The thing is, like it or not, we become adrenaline junkies after a while. That *can* affect our judgment. So just watch out for it. I found when I first came here that I had a tendency to magnify every symptom. If you're not careful, every cold can look like pneumonia or lung cancer or TB. I know that sounds like a stretch, but I've run that course. Sometimes still do. Where we've been, nothing was ever as simple as it looked at first glance. Now we're in a place where it most often *is* that simple."

"I can see that."

"I'm sure you can. Just remember, you've been conditioned to see things otherwise. Don't run on automatic. Ever."

With that, he picked up his charts and walked away, leaving her feeling as if, despite their friendlier conversation, she'd just been scolded again.

He had the *most* unfortunate manner, she decided. And was probably hypercritical, to judge by the way Julie and Nancy were trying to avoid him.

It was kind of funny, when she thought about it. Dr. David Marcus might have a bark, but at least he had the good grace to realize when he had crossed the line. And there were four other doctors in the joint practice that served the county and the hospital, so it wasn't as if he was the only one she'd be dealing with.

That was the point at which she realized that peace could have another downside. With only six patients on the ward, she actually had very little to do. There were only so many times she could disturb them by entering their rooms, only so many treatments and checks to be administered, and with a twelve-hour overnight shift yawning in front of her, she would need to make work to occupy herself.

Quite a change. Quite a change indeed. One thing Dr. Marcus had been right about: she was used to being on adrenaline most of the time. The cases on this ward shouldn't elevate her stress level by so much as a molecule.

A doer by nature, she decided to check the linen closet and supply closet for the routine needs of any hospital ward. She expected to find everything well-stocked, though. She wasn't the only night shift nurse to have time heavy on her hands.

As she was approaching the linen closet, an orderly emerged from the nearby cleaning closet with a cart, pail and mop. He seemed startled at her approach, then took a wide stance, as if planting himself firmly. A young man with tousled blond hair, a too-thin body and a narrow chin, he watched her approach almost warily. He looked to be fresh out of high school, which would have put him well out of her milieu when growing up, and the kindest word anyone would apply to his appearance was "ordinary." Poor guy probably had trouble getting dates.

"Hi," she said as she approached. "I'm Kristin Tate, the new night nurse." Something about him looked familiar, but then darn near everyone in the county looked familiar, even after all her time away.

"I recognize you," he said. Then, as if making a decision he added, "Charlie Waters. You probably don't remember me. We only talked a couple of times."

She smiled. "Sorry, I'm still getting to know everyone again. Nice to meet you. I was just wondering what I'm going to do all night. Any suggestions?"

A shy smile lit his face. "I play cards."

"Now that's an idea. Maybe the four of us can play."

"After I finish," he agreed.

"Do you have a deck of cards?"

He looked down at his scrubs as if to say, "Where would I be hiding them?"

"Good point," she said in response to his gesture. "I'll look through the drawers at the nurses' station. We can't be the only folks who have wondered how to get through a quiet night."

"Probably not," he agreed. "But I have a lot of work to do. Bathrooms and floors before the patients go to sleep. After that?"

"It's a date."

Julie and Nancy joined Krissie in her tallying of the supply closets, then returned to the nurses' station with her. No call lights, no monitor warnings. All the patients were happily watching TV or sleeping and, for the moment at least, experiencing no problems.

"It's awfully quiet tonight," Julie remarked.

Krissie perked at that. "You mean it's not usually like this?"

"Absolutely not," Nancy said. "We usually have a few more patients than this. More injuries, for one thing. And in August it's strange to have only one dehydration case."

"I'm not complaining," Julie remarked. "When the ward is full, we hardly get a breather."

"True that," Nancy agreed in the slang of the young.

Julie hesitated, then said, "I heard Dr. Marcus riding you. Not what he said but…just so you know, he can be hard to get along with sometimes."

Krissie wasn't quite sure how to respond. There were certain rules of professional etiquette, and while she'd seen them broken countless times when some doctor or nurse was a pain the rear, she didn't think she should encourage it her first night on the job.

But she didn't have to say a thing. Nancy chimed in. "I try to stay out of his way, because you never know when some little thing will annoy him. But mostly he's okay. I don't think he means to be edgy."

"I don't think so, either," Julie agreed. "Because he can be really nice sometimes. But other times, there's this look on his face, and you know he's uptight about something. So I just duck." She gave a little laugh. "If he's mad about something I did, he has to find me."

Krissie couldn't contain her smile. "Sometimes that works."

"Yeah, *you* can't really hide, being the charge nurse. Anyway, you'll find he's here a lot. The other docs all have families, so Dr. Marcus is on call most of the time." Julie scrunched her face a little. "Sometimes I think he doesn't sleep."

Or maybe, Krissie thought, *he has trouble sleeping.* She certainly did, even after all this time. Nightmares seemed ready to pounce, and were one of the reasons she preferred the night shift. When she had a nightmare while sleeping during the day, she only had to open her eyes to see sunlight, and she had learned it dispelled those images quickly. At least most of the time.

"Anyway," Nancy said, "it's probably the war."

Her comment was laden with the knowledgeable tone of someone who thought they knew. Krissie didn't think Nancy could imagine the half of it.

They did find a deck of cards, however, and after ten, when the patients had all been checked on, medicated and settled, Charlie joined them. He remained shy, but Julie seemed to have taken a shine to him, making him blush with alarming regularity.

Charlie left at midnight, his shift over, and Krissie sent Julie and Nancy to take a break. They announced they were going to the cafeteria to meet up with some friends from other wings and would be back in half an hour.

Krissie was amazed to discover how relieved she was to be left alone for a little while. The ward was quiet, the call board remained silent, Hester Alexander's heart monitor continued its steady rhythms.

One by one, she checked on her patients, moving soundlessly as she opened doors and looked in. Mr. Hedley was going to need a new IV bag of antibiotics in about an hour. Other than that, everyone seemed to be resting comfortably and sleeping deeply. Mrs. Alexander opened her watery blue eyes just briefly, then returned to sleep. Krissie silenced the monitor in her room. It was enough that she could keep an eye on it from the nurses' station; no need to disturb Mrs. Alexander's sleep.

The next couple of hours passed smoothly enough, and finally Krissie decided to take her own break, a half hour in the break room with her bagged lunch and another cup of coffee from the coffeemaker on the counter.

She had eaten only half of her turkey sandwich when her pager sounded. Julie. Dropping her sandwich on the waxed paper, she took off for the ward at a fast walk, just as the PA system announced a code and a room number.

She arrived a few seconds later on the ward to see Nancy waving at her from the door to Mrs. Alexander's room. From the nurses' station she heard the unmistakable warning from the cardiac monitor. Ignoring it, she began to jog down the hall, even though you were never supposed to run in a hospital.

"Cardiac arrest," Nancy said quietly. Inside the room, Julie was hovering over the patient looking helpless. Damn it, an LPN should know better.

"CPR, Julie. Did you call the doctor?"

Nancy nodded. "Yes. He answered the page."

"Julie, I'll take over. Where's the crash cart?"

"Getting it." Nancy fled.

Flatline. It was a sight a nurse saw too often, but never wanted to see. She joined Julie at the bed and motioned to her to take the breathing bag, while she herself climbed on the bed, straddled the patient and took over the chest compressions. Each compression registered on the monitor, but nothing else.

Dr. Marcus and the crash cart arrived together, along with a crash team assembled from all over the hospital. The high whine of the charging defibrillator filled the room along with business-like chatter as the team acted.

"Intubate."

Krissie paused in the compressions to allow the doctor to insert an endotracheal tube in the esophagus.

He worked swiftly, and moments later the breathing bag was attached to it, again worked by Julie.

"Two hundred," the doctor said, then to Krissie, "Off the bed." He was holding the paddles and Krissie quickly jumped down. "Clear!" he said, and applied the paddles.

Mrs. Alexander's body jumped, but the flatline remained.

"Push 20 ccs of sodium bicarb."

Another nurse stepped forward with a syringe. "Pushing."

"Give me three hundred."

A jolt of three hundred volts was applied, lifting the patient half off the bed. Still a flatline.

Krissie climbed back on the bed and continued compressions, counting automatically until Dr. Marcus said, "Clear."

She jumped down again and another shock was applied. Nothing.

"Epinephrine."

A large syringe was slapped into his hand, and Krissie watched as he stabbed the needle directly into the old lady's heart.

"Clear!"

Snap!

Nothing.

"Clear."

Snap!

Still that awful straight line…

"Compressions," Dr. Marcus said.

Krissie started to climb on the bed, but a male nurse beat her to it, giving her a break. Her arms were shaking. Her stomach turned upside down.

They called time of death at 3:31 a.m.

Chapter 2

David Marcus evidently had no desire to leave medical matters until morning. He sat at the nurses' station while orderlies worked in Mrs. Alexander's room, cleaning up the inevitable detritus of the code. In those moments where every second counted, items such as syringes and swabs went flying, along with their packaging. Mrs. Alexander herself lay carefully arranged beneath a sheet, awaiting whichever came first: a visit from immediate family or the trip to the morgue.

From moments of intense activity to absolute stillness. Krissie sat on a chair, staring at nothing. It didn't matter how many times she saw this, every time felt like a personal failure.

"There wasn't any warning?" David asked.

"I was in the break room eating my lunch when I got

the page. The code was called right after that. You'll have to check the monitor."

"Wasn't anyone watching it?"

"Julie or Nancy, I thought. But you can check and see if there was any warning."

His face tightened and he looked off into distant space. "She was getting better."

"That's how it looked."

"I guess we'll find out from the autopsy. But damn."

She managed a nod. "Why'd you push the bicarb?"

"Because she was on a potassium-sparing diuretic. There was a possibility that her kidneys hadn't cleared enough of it so it was one of the first things I thought of."

"I can see that."

"Except that tests didn't show anything wrong with her kidneys."

"Things change." Krissie rubbed her eyes, trying to hold back a tidal wave of despair. Before long, the second-guessing would set in. It always did and seldom helped. A lot of medical people, herself included, belonged to a secret society of flagellants, beating themselves up when they lost a patient they felt they shouldn't have. Given another half hour, she'd probably be telling herself it was all her fault for taking a break.

"Damn it, David, we both know how fast things can change. She'd evidently had a heart attack in the past. Hence the arrhythmia that caused the congestive heart failure."

"I *know* that," he snapped. "And I was treating all of that. The arrhythmia, the edema…"

"I know." She almost snapped back.

"Maybe I shouldn't have cut so much diuretic."

Krissie shook her head. "That change shouldn't have caused such a big effect so fast."

"No, you're right."

Astonished that he had so quickly accepted her judgment after snapping at her, she blinked and stared at him.

He turned to the monitor and hit the buttons to play back the hour before the attack.

"Coffee?" Krissie asked finally. Every nerve in her body seemed to be firing. "I can't just sit here."

"Sure. Thanks. Black, please."

Forcing herself to stand, she walked back toward the nurses' break room. She didn't want to wonder if things might have been different if she hadn't gone on break, if Julie and Nancy hadn't been so obviously overtaken by the enormity of what they were facing. Training. She'd need to give them more training. They were little more than kids, really.

And none of those thoughts helped. A woman had died, and no one in the medical profession would ever be comfortable with that outcome if there was the remotest possibility they might have prevented it.

She filled two cups, paused to look at her sandwich, then, realizing she wouldn't be able to eat it, swept the remains into the trash.

Back at the ward, she found David peering intently at the monitor. "There it is," he said, when she came up and put the coffee beside him.

"What?"

"See that? Major slowdown. Like it just wound down."

"Arrhythmia?"

"For about fifteen seconds before the slowdown. Easy enough to miss. The monitor should have alarmed."

"Maybe it did. It was screeching when I got here, and Julie and Nancy were in the patient's room."

He nodded slowly. "It was fast."

She scanned the playback as he ran through it again. "Awfully fast."

"Looks more like SCA, sudden cardiac arrest."

Krissie nodded. "Not much time to do anything."

"No." He lowered his head for a moment. "I need to call her family."

The worst task of all, Krissie thought. "I'll talk to Julie and Nancy, see if I can learn anything additional. For the report."

He nodded. "Thanks. God knows what I'm going to tell the family." He pushed forward on the ECG readout, then said, "It's clear compressions were started in about a minute." The spikes showed that clearly. "You weren't too late."

It struck her then that he was trying to let her know she couldn't have done any more. His generosity, when he was sitting there blaming himself, was all the more touching. And totally unexpected after the way they had started.

"David—"

He cut her off. "I need to call the family." He rose and strode away, looking lonely as only a doctor at a time like this could.

The phlebotomist emerged from Mrs. Alexander's room with his cart, trundling all the blood samples to the lab. Moments later the orderlies came out, carrying away trash, pushing the crash cart with them to restock it and prepare it for another code. Then came Julie and Nancy, both with hanging heads.

"We messed up," Nancy said as they joined Julie behind the counter and sat. "We called the code and called you, but we should have started CPR."

"Yes, you should have." But Krissie took pity on them, too. "I was there in less than a minute. Compressions started soon enough anyway."

They nodded. "We never had anyone die before," Julie said softly. "Never."

Krissie looked at them, not knowing quite what to say. "It never gets any easier," she managed finally. "Now just make sure Mrs. Alexander is ready to be seen by her family. I'm going to check on the other patients. If any of them awoke, they're probably disturbed by this. Tomorrow, we'll talk about managing these events a little better."

Rising, she touched their shoulders in turn. "We learn from our mistakes. I still do. But there was nothing you could have done that would have saved her."

The two girls nodded, but neither looked particularly relieved.

To her dismay, she found the boy with the broken leg, Tom Mason, wide awake and looking frightened. He was only ten. "Am I going to die, too?"

"Of course not!" Krissie pulled a chair closer to his bed. "You're young and healthy. The person who died was very old and sick. There's a difference."

He nodded and allowed her to pat his hand as she sat beside him.

"I know it's scary for you," she said calmly. "It's scary for everyone. But you don't even have a heart monitor, which should tell you something."

"Okay."

She waited, giving him space to talk, to say whatever he needed to, but he remained quiet, as if trying to sort through things in his own mind his own way.

"Look," she said presently, "Some people are sick and come to hospitals to die. Others, like you, just managed to break their legs jumping out of a tree, and they come here to get better. Before you know it, you're going to be hobbling around on crutches and asking your friends to sign your cast. Just tell them not to use dirty words."

At that, a shy smile peeped out. "Mom would be furious."

"You better believe it. She'll probably go get a can of white paint to cover it up. And what if she just keeps painting the rest of you?"

A tired little laugh escaped him. "She'd paint my bottom, and it wouldn't be with a paintbrush."

Krissie forced a grin. "You think she'd spank you?"

He shook his head after a minute. "She never hits me. She doesn't have to."

"Oh," Krissie said knowingly. "The *mother* voice."

"Yeah. And Dad says her looks can kill."

"Oh, I know all about that. My mother never spanked me, either, but one look and I'd practically burst into flames or something."

"I go hide. I hate it when she's mad at me."

"Somehow I think she doesn't get mad at you often."

"No," he said with confidence. "I'm pretty good most of the time."

"I believe you."

He looked at her from the corner of his eye. "But she *was* mad when I jumped out of that tree. Especially when she saw my leg."

"Probably more worried than mad."

"Yeah, that's what she said later."

"Do you want me to call your mom, ask her to come in?"

He hesitated, then shook his head. "I'm okay. You're right. I'm not old and sick."

"No, you're not." She headed for the door, but when she got there, his voice stopped her.

"Can you leave the door open?"

She smiled back at him. "Sure. And why don't you turn on the light on your bed and read one of those comic books. But don't turn the TV on, okay? Not with the door open."

"Okay." He reached for a comic book from one of the stacks on the table beside the bed and flipped on the fluorescent light at the head of the bed. "Thanks, Miss Tate."

"Just call me Krissie, okay? Can I get you anything? A drink? Jell-O?"

"I'm okay. Thanks."

"Use that call button if you want anything."

"I will." At that he grinned, then turned his attention to the comic book.

Am I going to die, too? Outside, Krissie had to stop and lean against the wall, closing her eyes and reaching for balance. How many times had she heard that question from boys only a few years older than this one? From men, women and children. And how many times had she had to lie about it?

Am I going to die, too? The question haunted her nightmares. Bloody hands gripping her arm. Shattered bodies, shattered faces, shattered lives. Death riding her shoulder as if he were her partner.

God!

After a minute, she regained her equilibrium and was able to continue her ward check. Everyone else still slept, apparently unaware the grim reaper had paid a visit.

Mrs. Alexander's son—a rawboned man who looked as if he had worked hard outdoors his entire life—arrived and went into the room with David, then emerged ten minutes later by himself, walking away with a tight jaw and reddened eyes. David came out a minute later and approached the station.

"She can go to the morgue now. They don't want an autopsy."

"But…"

"I told him we needed to do one anyway, to find out what happened. He said he doesn't care what happened. It's enough she's gone, let her be."

Krissie nodded slowly.

"We got the blood samples and we have the urine bag, right?"

"Yes, I saw the lab guys take it all."

"Okay, then. We'll have to rely on toxicology, a BUN test, the other tests I ordered. It'll probably be enough."

She understood, though. He wanted to know *exactly* what had gone wrong, and if the blood and urine tests didn't show anything, questions would plague him for a long time.

He reached for the now-cold cup of coffee he'd left on the desk an hour ago and drank it down. Then he gave her a kind of cockeyed smile. "That was awful."

"I can get you fresh."

"Tell you what. Let me buy you breakfast at Maude's. You get off at seven, right?"

"Right." Part of her hesitated, saying *no, this would be stupid,* but another part didn't want to go straight home, not after this night. "It's a deal. I'll meet you there as soon as I get out of here."

"Deal. A little artery-hardening food is what I need right now." Then, with a nod, he left.

The sun was already well up and growing hot when Krissie left the hospital shortly after seven. Dressed again in her street clothes, carrying her small backpack, she walked across the pavement to her car. Her eyes felt gritty, a sure sign she needed some sleep, but she'd toughed this out before countless times. Impatiently, she ran her fingers through her short, streaked hair.

As she started to pull out of the parking lot, a small wave of panic washed over her and she almost turned for home rather than downtown and Maude's diner.

This was purely professional, she told herself. Two colleagues getting together to eat and unwind a bit before going home to bed. There was nothing to be afraid of.

But her recently defunct relationship had left its own set of scars, among them her fear and dislike of controlling men. That little outburst from David last night about his expectations of her as a nurse had been controlling. She still squirmed a little when she thought about it, but reminded herself that he hadn't behaved that way during their encounters the rest of the night. Still, he had the potential to become a problem of the kind she had just shucked.

But only if she let him, she reminded herself. Keep it professional, keep it purely social and don't let him get close. That was a recipe for avoiding trouble, one she intended to follow.

Feeling more comfortable about it, she found a parking space near Maude's and walked the rest of the way to the diner. For some reason, Maude had added a Café sign to her window, even though the neon above announced City Diner. Not that it mattered, she supposed. Everyone still called it Maude's, or Maude's Diner.

Inside, wonderful aromas filled the air, and the clanking of flatware and the clatter of crockery joined the hum of early-morning conversation. Like many such places, the early-morning weekday crowd was composed mostly of older people, men, women and couples, who had no need to think about getting ready to go to work. Later in the day, the composition would change, first with the lunch crowd, then the dinner crowd.

David stood out: a man in his prime, maybe around forty, with dark hair that didn't yet show a dash of gray. In his dark blue polo shirt and khaki slacks, he looked lithe and fit. He'd taken a table near the window and already had a cup of coffee in front of him. He started to get up as she approached, but she waved him back into his seat and then slid onto the vinyl-covered chair facing him.

Before she had a chance to say a word, a cup slammed onto the table in front of her and started to fill with coffee. She looked up and saw Maude's daughter, Mabel; the younger woman was surely a clone of her mother.

"Good to see you back, Krissie," Mable said as she topped off the mugs. "Menu? Or do you know what you want?"

Krissie knew better than to ask for anything unusual

or healthful. This wasn't a place for healthful eating. "Two-egg onion omelet and rye toast, please."

Mabel nodded, then looked at David. "The usual?"

"Please. With some extra hash browns."

"Got it." Mabel sort of smiled and walked away, coffee carafe in hand.

Krissie smiled. "You're going for broke."

"The hash browns, you mean? Yeah. I need every calorie I can get. I still have office hours, starting at nine."

"You should be catching a nap then."

"I couldn't sleep right now."

She looked down at her coffee, then across at him again. "I would have thought you'd have learned to sleep anytime, anywhere."

"Because of being military?" He shrugged. "That used to be easier. You might not understand this yet, I don't know. But the losses are harder now. Maybe because the patients aren't usually in such a bad state."

Krissie nodded slowly. "I guess I can see that."

"Maybe you won't feel that way. I hope not."

"Too early to tell. So what's your background?"

He sipped his coffee as if buying time to consider what he should say.

"Oh, come on," she prodded. "You read *my* jacket. Fair's fair."

At that, he smiled. "Okay. I enlisted at eighteen, became a medic in time for Desert Storm. Bad enough, but I was still on fire with the desire to be able to do more to help, so eventually I went to college, got admitted to medical school. The army picked up the tab on my medical training in return for a six-year commitment. It was mostly okay. Until Iraq."

"Yeah."

"Same for you?"

She shook her head, biting her upper lip. "Not quite. I went to nursing school on scholarship and enlisted after I got my B.S. in nursing. The navy trained me to be a nurse practitioner, and the next thing I knew, I was in Asia on the USS *Hope* after the tsunami."

"My God, that must have been awful."

"Not my favorite memory. But after that, I was attached to the Marine Corps and served in Iraq."

"In the field," he said as if it weren't a question.

"In the field," she agreed. "Well, at bases with field hospitals."

"Yeah, the ones they pretend aren't at the front line."

She lifted her gaze and saw understanding there. A wealth of understanding. "There is no front line."

He nodded. "Exactly."

Mabel returned and slapped their plates down in front of them. Krissie stared at hers, certain there had to be more than two eggs in that omelet. Plus there were hash browns she hadn't asked for and *four* slices of rye toast.

David must have read her expression. He laughed. "I think Maude thinks you're too thin."

"Maude thinks everyone is too thin."

Krissie glanced toward the window and caught sight of her reflection. She *was* a little under her fighting weight, and worse, she suddenly realized that the blond streaks in her light brown hair were growing out to the point that they no longer looked good. She experienced a moment of self-consciousness, then quickly dismissed it. She'd only applied those streaks because Alvin had insisted on it. He'd wanted her to go completely blond, but at least she'd managed to draw that line. Of course, with Al, it was his way or the highway. It had taken a while, but she'd finally chosen the highway.

Whatever had possessed her to stay for so long?

"Penny for your thoughts?"

David's voice drew her back, and she looked at him. "Nothing," she said. "Just a memory."

"And thoughts are worth a lot more than a penny these days."

David could be charming, she realized. That concerned her as much as their initial encounter. Control and charm had gone hand-in-hand with Alvin. Just like that, she went on high alert.

"What's wrong?" David asked.

Perceptive, too. "Nothing," she said firmly and turned her attention to her overburdened plate. Just the sight of all that food made her feel full, but she hadn't eaten a bite. And since she hadn't eaten her lunch during her break, she knew she was going to have to tuck in or get sick later.

She picked up a slice of toast, already buttered by the prodigious purveyor of fatty food herself, Maude, and took a bite. At least her stomach didn't revolt. In fact, once the toast reached bottom, she began to feel hungry. A sip of coffee took care of the last of her revulsion.

David tucked in, too, and for a while, they ate in silence.

The tragic mood of the night began to give way to life. One of the hardest and fastest lessons medical people had to learn was that life went on even when someone died. That they weren't God, and sometimes had to just let go. Clinging to their losses only made them less capable of caring for the next patient.

But neither could they afford to grow hard. No, they just had to quick-time their way through the sense of failure and loss to be ready for the next case.

David spoke. "So you worked in the VA hospital in Denver, right?"

She tensed immediately. "Yes. I did."

He looked at her. "Bad topic?"

She half shrugged. "Well, it was emotionally tough. Easier in some ways than Iraq, harder in others."

"I would think so. At one end, you're focused on saving a life. At the other, you're looking at the destruction left in the wake of it."

"You can never do enough. And the vast majority of the patients I had were amazingly positive, considering what they faced. Oh, they got angry at times, and depressed, but by and large, they handled it better than I did."

"How so?"

She hesitated. "Well…sometimes I found myself furious. Because we saved them for this? A life without limbs, a life with brain damage, a life of paralysis? And every time it started to overwhelm me, some patient would say he was glad he'd made it." She shook her head and closed her eyes for a minute. "Sorry."

"No, I'm sorry. I shouldn't have brought it up. The whole point of dragging you here for breakfast was to get some calories into the two of us and shuck what happened so we can get on with what comes next." He looked rueful. "So, idiot that I am, I stick my foot right in it."

She had to smile, and made a major effort to shake off the memories. "I guess we all get our scars."

"So your dad used to be sheriff here?"

She almost laughed at the pointed change of subject. "Yeah. Forever, it seems. Certainly since before I was born. Deep roots in these parts."

"I haven't really had a chance to get to know him yet."

"You will. Retired or not, this county belongs to Dad." She grinned. "Or so he thinks. He's keeping his hand in, one way or another. Small ways. It must be driving Gage nuts."

"Gage? You mean the new sheriff, Gage Dalton?"

"Yup. And note the way you say 'the new sheriff.' He's been doing it for three years now, and everyone still says he's the new sheriff."

David chuckled. "That could get annoying."

"Gage doesn't seem to mind. He's either a really good actor, or he has his priorities straight."

"I don't really know him, either. I don't have a whole lot of contact with the sheriff's department."

"Well, we'll have to change that. It's the best way to get wired into the county. You probably know my sister, though. Wendy Yuma, the flight nurse with the emergency response team."

"She's your sister? I know her all right, her and Billy Joe. Great people."

"Maybe we should all get together some time." As soon as she said it, she wanted to withdraw the suggestion. How much better did she really want to know this edgy, possibly difficult man? He might want to forget he'd come on like gangbusters at their first meeting, but she wouldn't. Couldn't afford to. She'd had enough of control freaks to last her a lifetime.

"Yeah, that could be fun."

He went back to eating, obviously blessed with a healthy appetite as well as dark good looks. But as she sat there, nibbling at her toast and omelet, Krissie realized the man didn't look happy at all. Either last night was still upsetting him, or he carried a load of garbage even bigger than hers.

Which wouldn't be surprising. You didn't come out of a war without garbage. Tons of it. Not if you were human.

But she didn't want to go there. Not now. Maybe not ever. Even thinking about the VA hospital upset her, so how could she talk about what they'd both seen in Iraq? Sometimes it was better to let sleeping dogs lie.

Finally, Krissie simply couldn't eat another bite. She pushed her plate to one side, expecting Maude or Mabel to come give her the standard lecture about wasting good food. Instead, Mabel didn't say a word. She simply refilled their mugs with fresh coffee and took the plate away.

Maybe, Krissie thought with a burst of inner humor, miracles still happened.

David suddenly spoke. "You look exhausted. Why don't you go get some sleep? I'll get the bill. My treat."

As soon as he spoke, she realized he was right. She was too exhausted to manage a conversation about even something as inane as the weather.

"I *am* tired," she admitted.

"I can see that." He lifted one corner of his mouth in a smile. "Go rest up. I'm sure I'll see you tonight."

"Tonight?" That rattled her, then she remembered. "Oh, yeah. Tonight. I'm on shift."

He nodded, and his smile widened. "Definitely exhausted. Off with you. See you later."

She was strangely glad to escape the normally pleasant sounds and smells of the diner and climbed into her little car with relief.

The night was over. So much for peace.

Chapter 3

Afternoon sunlight slanted through Krissie's bedroom window, a welcome sight as she awoke. She smiled and stretched contentedly. The air mattress beneath her made its familiar hollow sounds.

Being in the navy for six years had taught her to minimize her possessions. If it didn't fit in a duffel bag, she didn't own it. Then the habit proved hard to break, and the few items of furniture she had bought while working in Denver had seemed easier to sell than to move.

She needed to change that mindset, she thought now. A bed, a table, some additional cooking utensils, maybe even a sofa. She could afford these things from her savings, and since she was determined to stay here now that she had come home, she didn't need to live like a gypsy any more.

In fact, she thought ruefully, gypsies probably had more worldly possessions. She stretched again and glanced at the small travel alarm clock near her bed. Four o'clock already! She must have slept like the dead.

Just time enough to grab a shower and try to make something to eat, then pack a lunch for her shift. And maybe a quick chat with Mom on the phone.

Almost as if reading her mind, her cell phone rang, and she saw her parents' phone number pop up. Smiling, she opened the phone and answered.

"Hi," she said.

"Hi, honey." Her mother's warm voice filled her ear. "I hope I didn't wake you."

"I was just waking up."

"Oh, goodie. So, you know what the best thing about having you back in town is?" Marge Tate's tone became gently humorous.

"No, what?"

"I can ask you over for dinner now. And it just so happens we decided to eat early. That wouldn't have anything to do with the fact you have to be back on shift at seven."

Krissie laughed. "Oh, Mom!"

"So your dad's heating up the grill and I thought we'd make burgers, and I'm in the middle of making this really great salad—"

"Sold!" Krissie said. "I just need to shower and throw some things together for tonight."

"Don't rush, honey. Dinner won't be until five or so. But while you're not rushing, hurry up. I miss you."

Still smiling, Krissie closed her phone, jumped up and trotted to the shower. God, it was good to be home!

The Tate family house looked as it always had during the years Krissie and the five other girls had grown up there, except that it had a fresh coat of white paint and some new bushes out front. The full-size van was gone, too, no longer necessary for carting six kids around.

But it was still home, and as soon as Krissie stepped through the front door, she felt enveloped in warmth and love.

She found her parents out back on the deck, sipping tall glasses of lemonade. Immediately, they enveloped her in hugs, as if they hadn't just seen her two days ago, then sat her down with her own glass of lemonade.

Nate, her dad, didn't look a day older than he had when she left for the navy eight years ago. It was as if he'd weathered and aged all he could by forty, and then remained unchanging.

Marge had put on a couple of pounds, but on her they looked good. She had apparently stopped washing her short hair with henna, so the red had faded mostly to gray. The years, however, had taken no toll on her smile or her twinkling eyes.

"We invited Wendy and Billy Joe for dinner, too," Marge said, "but apparently there was a car accident, so you're stuck with just us for company."

"As if I'd complain?"

Nate chuckled, a deep gravelly sound. "Well, I know how much you were looking forward to the three-ring circus."

"No, that's Christmas, when everyone comes home."

Nate laughed again. "My favorite time of year."

Marge smiled at him. "Go get the burgers, dear. Krissie has limited time and I want to have a private word."

"Uh-oh," Krissie said humorously as her dad rose from his chair.

He leaned over and dropped a kiss on her forehead. "Call me if you need protection."

"Oh, go on," Marge laughed. "It's nothing like that."

Nate disappeared through the sliding glass door, closing it pointedly behind him.

Marge looked at Krissie as if drinking in every detail. "I know you wrote and called all the time while you were away. But I'm a mother, and I can tell there was a lot you weren't saying."

"Mom…"

Marge shook her head and patted her hand. "Nate says I shouldn't ask, and he would know. I just want you to know that if you ever need to talk, I'm here."

"I've always known that." But Krissie felt her throat tighten anyway, and she had to swallow hard.

"And if you feel it's something only your dad would understand, well, he's here, too."

"I know…" Krissie could hardly talk around the sudden lump in her throat. Marge left her chair to come wrap her arms tightly around her daughter. All of a sudden, Krissie felt like a small child again, when all the comfort in the world could be found within the arms of her mother, with her head on her mother's breast. Comfort and safety.

"I can only imagine," Marge murmured. "I can only imagine. But you'll heal now. I know you will."

"I'm healing already," Krissie managed, her voice thick.

"Yes, you are. I knew it when you decided to come home."

Marge squeezed her hard then let go. As if reading a signal, Nate returned with a plate of raw burgers.

"I hope you're hungry," he said jovially. "'Cuz I'm cooking for four."

Marge resumed her seat, raising a brow. "He's always looking for an excuse to get a second burger."

"Well, if you'd let me have them more often, I wouldn't need to resort to tricks!"

Krissie laughed, feeling the intense emotions begin to subside, allowing her to breathe and swallow again. "I love you guys," she said.

Her answer came in unison, "We love you, too."

When Krissie arrived at the hospital just before seven, she realized the auto accident must have been a serious one. Police cars and two ambulances stood at the emergency room entrance, and the medevac helicopter was on the pad not far away. Even as she walked across the parking lot, she saw her sister Wendy emerge alongside a gurney headed for the helicopter, an IV bag swinging in the breeze. The rotors were powering up even before the gurney reached the chopper.

Taking a chance, she entered by way of the E.R. and was collared immediately by David. "We need you here," he said briskly. "Have someone call the ward and tell the charge nurse not to leave."

"What happened?"

"Three-car pileup. One of them was a van with a family of five."

Krissie nodded and took off. She called the ward herself to advise them she'd be late, then tore to the changing room to pull on scrubs and booties. Back out in the E.R. controlled chaos reigned. To a practiced eye, it was clear that everything was functioning as it should, even though they were shorthanded, but to the uneducated, it probably looked like total uproar.

"In here." David motioned her into a cubicle and she found a child of maybe eight or nine on the gurney inside. He was unconscious, but breathing normally. David bent over him, ignoring the blood, and began to listen to chest sounds, then to palpate.

"I don't see any wounds," he said. "Do you?"

Krissie immediately stepped in and began to check the small body from head to toe. "Head gash," she said. "Already stopped bleeding. Maybe two stitches, nothing major."

"Got it."

She kept working her way downward, checking limbs, searching every inch of skin. "Nothing else. Either he bled heavily for a while or it's someone else's blood."

David finished putting two sutures in the scalp wound. "Check BP again, make sure it's not falling."

She pressed the button on the automatic blood pressure machine and watched the cuff inflate then release. "Good BP," she said, scanning the readout.

"Good. Send him on to X-ray. No way to tell what's broken, but make sure they do a good job on the head."

But before they could take him away, David stopped them and looked at the boy's abdomen again. What he saw made him pause. "Seat belt."

Krissie stepped closer and watched David trace the faint outline of an emerging bruise. As soon as she saw it, she turned back to the BP monitor and took another reading. "Steady," she said. But as she turned back to David, she saw the worry in his eyes. They both knew

what a seat belt could do in an accident: ruptured
spleen, other organ damage from sudden pressure. The
damage might be small right now, too small to detect
with palpation, but if allowed to go untreated, it could
become a death sentence.

"You go with him," David told her. "Monitor constantly. But we need those X-rays."

"Yes, doctor."

So, keeping the child hooked up to his IV, and with
the blood pressure monitor tucked onto the bed with
him, Krissie helped push the gurney to X-ray. "What's
his name?" she called over her shoulder.

David shook his head. "No names yet."

"Tell the cops I need to know."

"I will." He was already moving on to the next
patient. A woman suddenly screamed, but not even that
woke the boy.

"Poor little tyke," said the orderly helping her to
push the gurney. For the first time, Krissie looked up
and saw Charlie Waters.

"Oh, hi, Charlie. Sorry, I was focused on the boy."

He nodded. "Everyone is focused right now."

Two X-ray technicians were already waiting. Krissie
insisted on remaining at the boy's bedside, so she
donned a lead apron. As they moved his little body
around so they could get an unobstructed view of every
bone in his body, she found herself grateful that, for
now at least, he remained unconscious. If any of those
bones were broken, this would have been hell on earth
for him, and he'd already been through quite enough.

A radiologist had been called in, and he began ex-
amining the X-rays as they developed, before the entire
set was even taken. Krissie kept checking the blood

pressure, and every few minutes, palpated the child's abdomen. No sign that it was hardening, even though the seat-belt bruise was becoming more apparent.

The radiologist joined her before they were even done. "He needs to be transported," he said. "There's a compression fracture in his left skull. It's not deep, not something you'd probably find by touch, but he needs an MRI stat."

That was all Krissie needed to hear. Small hospital, no MRI available. It was one of those things you dealt with here. "Call down to E.R. and tell Dr. Marcus, will you? We'll get him out as fast as we can."

The radiologist nodded and waved them on their way. Another gurney, holding a moaning man, was already waiting in line.

By the time they returned to the emergency room, another helicopter was landing, this one from a neighboring county. The boy was rushed on board, along with a woman who seemed to be wavering in and out of consciousness. Instructions were given, then Krissie, Charlie and David stood back as the helicopter lifted to the sky.

"God," said David, "some days I hate being at a small hospital."

"Yeah." Krissie could understand his frustration. With something like this, every minute counted, and because they didn't have all the bells and whistles, the minutes were stacking up.

Then she looked into David's eyes, and saw the same ghosts that must be in her own. He visibly shook himself and started back to the E.R. She and Charlie followed.

"Maybe," she heard David mutter, "we need to start a fund-raising drive for some new equipment."

"I'll help," Krissie said promptly.

He looked at her, appearing slightly embarrassed. "That wasn't meant for general distribution."

"I know. But it's still true."

"Stabilize and transport usually works."

"I know." And she did. That's mostly what they'd had to do in field hospitals. Even in major metropolitan areas, only one or two hospitals were equipped as trauma centers. Stabilize and transport was a medical dictum in many places, because it was the only efficient way to use resources.

An hour later, they'd cleared the accident victims. Two had gone to surgery, two had been moved to the general ward, the rest had been transported. Krissie hurried to take a shower and change into clean scrubs before going up to relieve the day-shift charge nurse.

Denise Albright greeted her like a savior. A small woman with surprisingly broad shoulders, she had pretty gray eyes and a huge smile. "Girl, am I glad to see you! My feet are screaming."

"Been busy?"

"You wouldn't believe. I guess the last week was the calm before the storm. In addition to the two accident victims you already know about, we got four more."

"What's going on?"

Denise grinned. "The usual. Accidents. You shouldn't stand on the edge of the bathtub to change a light bulb."

Krissie compressed her lips to stifle a laugh. "New rule."

"Definitely. Lucky it was only a broken arm and a concussion. Then we have Mr. I-got-careless-with-the-farm-equipment. He needed twenty-nine stitches, a unit of blood and is on IV antibiotics. We have a first-degree burn case which is highly painful and resulted from splashing grease. New rule: watch it when you dump those frozen fries into a big pot of very hot grease. She'll be okay, she was lucky to be standing back far enough for the grease to cool some, but the pain is enough that she's on some powerful meds, so she needs watching. Also, they said she seemed a little shocky when she came in."

"Got it. And the last one?"

"Now this is my very favorite." Denise paused for effect.

"Another new rule?"

"Yup. When you get mad at your husband, don't punch your arm through a plate-glass window."

"Oh, my gosh!"

"Two units of blood, seventeen stitches, IV antibiotics and an emergency restraining order. I doubt she'll get any visitors tonight. No one has showed up so far."

"I'd be worried about who would."

At that, Denise laughed. "Yeah. Anyway, Julie and Nancy are making the rounds, so you have time to read the files and get up to speed. Me, I'm off. I need my supper. See you tomorrow!"

Krissie settled in to read all the files, finding pretty much what Denise had told her. Except, the burn patient niggled at her. Linda Nelson had been admitted by Dr. Randolph at 4:30 p.m. with extensive first-degree burns on her stomach and abdomen, and a much smaller second-degree burn on her arm. The wounds had not been inspected since they had been treated and bandaged.

At once, she left the nurses' station and went to find Linda Nelson. The thing about burns, even first-degree burns, is that when they first presented, you didn't always see all the damage. Also, more damage could appear later and the body sometimes produced an immune reaction to burns, which could make them worsen.

Everyone had been busy with the mess in the E.R. so it wasn't surprising that the nurses had forgotten to check the burns again.

She found Linda groggy from morphine, but still conscious. "It hurts," the patient said plaintively.

"Burns are the worst," Krissie said sympathetically.

"You've seen a lot?"

"Too many." Another mental image to shove out of the way. "I'm going to check them, okay? Someone needs to look every so often."

"Will it hurt more?"

"I'll be as gentle as I can, I promise. Sometimes though, when the air hits a burn, the pain can spike a little."

Linda bit her lower lip, then nodded. "I get more morphine soon, right?"

"As soon as I can give it to you. I won't forget."

"Okay." She screwed her eyes shut. "God, I can't believe I was so stupid. But Tommy screamed just as I was starting to pour the fries into the pot."

"Tommy?"

"My four-year-old. I guess Sally, his older sister, accidentally hit him in the head with a ball…. I don't know. He just screamed, and I jumped."

"Accidents happen," Krissie said soothingly. Gently, she opened the woman's gown and began to ease the huge gauze pad away. "I know you, don't I?"

"Maybe." Linda drew a sharp breath. "I was six

years behind you in school, but everybody knew you because you were the sheriff's daughter."

"That was a curse, I can tell you."

"I bet. Every bit as bad as being the preacher's kid, probably." Linda winced and gasped.

"I'm sorry." She was even more sorry when she saw the reddened skin beneath the gauze. Widespread blistering had begun. Gently she laid the pad down. "I'm going to get the doctor in, okay? But first let me check whether you're due for more morphine."

"God, I hope so! I swear, it's hurting worse."

"It probably feels that way. Must be time for another shot."

It was. She administered the morphine immediately through the IV port, then promised to come back in ten minutes.

Outside Linda's door, Krissie saw Julie coming down the hall. "Stay with Mrs. Nelson while I get the doctor. Put her on the monitor and watch for shock."

Julie's eyes widened a hair. "Got it. What's going on?"

"The burns are deepening."

"Oh, no." Julie's step quickened, and she entered the room with a squeak of rubbery soles.

Krissie hurried down to the nurses' station and paged the physician on duty. Of course it was David.

"What's up?" he asked on the phone.

"We've got a burn patient up here. Randolph admitted her with first-degree burns of the abdomen and stomach. I just looked and she's blistering badly."

"I'm on my way."

She couldn't hold it back then. Closing her eyes, she leaned against the counter while memories washed over her in Technicolor horror. Burns of every kind and description, burns of men, women and children, burns so bad you couldn't believe the victim still breathed. At its very heart, war *burned*.

A touch yanked her back from the precipice. She opened her eyes and saw David.

"Are you okay?" he asked.

"Burns," she answered. It was all she could say.

His face darkened. "I know. God, do I know. Which room? You stay here if you need to."

Sympathy from the devil. A crazy thought that just popped into her mind. David Marcus was no devil. No, there were real devils out there.

Gathering herself, she followed him to check on Linda. Julie sat beside the bed, the monitor had been connected, and the patient's blood pressure, a tad low, was still okay.

David spoke a few words, then leaned over Linda. "Is the morphine helping?"

"The new shot is."

"Good…good." Carefully, he lifted the bandage and looked. Then he lowered it. "Linda?"

"Yes?"

"The burns are a little worse than Dr. Randolph thought when he first saw them. I'm not saying he was wrong, this just happens sometimes. We can't always tell right off how bad they are."

Linda's eyes opened a bit wider. "Worse? What does that mean?"

David took her hand and squeezed gently. "I think we're going to need to move you to a burn treatment center."

"Oh, God!"

"Shh…shh…" So gentle. "It's going to be okay. Really. But we can't do enough here to make you comfortable. You're starting to blister. So you need someone who can do everything necessary to get you well fast. Faster than we can here. We just don't have all the equipment and the kind of expertise you'll find at a burn center."

A tear ran down Linda's cheek. "Who'll take care of my kids?"

"Your husband can make arrangements. Family? A friend? We'll help you get that sorted out first." He glanced at Krissie.

She stepped forward and smiled. "Of course we'll make sure your kids will be taken care of. How about I call my mom? She'll see to it."

The tiniest of smiles lifted the corner of Linda's mouth. "That I believe." But then her smile wavered and more tears fell. "How bad is it?"

David never hesitated. "I've seen a lot worse. It's just that, with the blistering, we have to start worrying about infection." He didn't mention the likelihood of skin grafts. She didn't need to hear that right now.

"Okay," she said weakly. "Can you call my husband?"

"Right now," Krissie promised. "Right now."

"I want to see him before I go."

"I'll tell him."

Then the morphine carried her away.

Chapter 4

"Tough night, huh?"

Krissie looked up in surprise as David entered the break room. The ward had settled for the night, and now, in the wee hours, she was trying to find any desire at all to eat the tuna sandwich she'd packed earlier, and drink her coffee. David was the last person she expected to see.

"Don't you ever sleep?" she asked.

"Do you?"

She caught the drift. "Sometimes I even manage it without nightmares."

"Yeah." He poured a coffee and sat across the table from her. "I had a friend years ago. He was a priest."

She waited, staring at her sandwich. Just last night, this man had berated her the instant he clapped eyes on her. Now tonight, he was treating her with trust and even friendship. Unfortunately, when you put those two things together, you might be looking at trouble, at a natural-born manipulator. She couldn't trust him yet, and probably never would. But she could listen anyway.

"Anyway, this friend of mine never seemed to sleep. All day long he was doing his priestly thing, and then at night he would ride with ambulances to help out. I thought he was a man with a huge need to help people."

"But?" She looked at him.

"I figured it all out a few years later when he left the priesthood. He was a man running from demons."

She nodded slowly. "Want half of my sandwich?"

"No, I'm fine. And you need to eat."

"I already have a mother."

He chuckled. "I've met her. You better eat."

Whatever her other thoughts, Krissie had to smile at that.

"So," he said, "is that why you took the night shift?"

She frowned at him. "Is that why *you're* always here?"

"Touché." He continued to smile faintly. "You did good catching that burn."

"I've seen a lot of burns."

"I know."

She met his gaze then, and once again saw echoes of her own demons.

He leaned forward a little. "Is this what you expected when you came here?"

"How so?"

"That you'd feel helpless?"

"I've been feeling essentially helpless for a long time."

He stared at her, then nodded. "I know. When I was a corpsman I kept thinking that if only I was a doctor I could do more. Then I discovered I can do more but it doesn't always help."

"Yeah."

"I had to get out of trauma. I think you know what I mean. There's just so much you can take, even on adrenaline. So I come to this little hospital, thinking I'll be practicing the better side of medicine, the tummy aches, the broken arms, all the little things that life dishes out, and I'll get to know my patients as families."

"And have you?"

"To some extent, it's exactly what I wanted. Then we have a night like tonight and I feel my hands are tied behind my back, and I reach for equipment that isn't there, and want to order tests I can't and…" He shrugged. "Nights like tonight are a different kind of nightmare, that's all."

She completely understood. An ache squeezed her heart, as she realized he was talking to her because she had a similar background. There probably weren't a whole lot of people in the county who'd seen the war from inside a medical unit. Unfortunately, she hadn't gotten far enough past her own problems to offer much help.

Finally, she said the only thing that occurred to her. "Maybe there's a difference in degree and quantity."

He nodded as if he were weighing her evaluation. "Perhaps that's it. Most nights aren't like tonight."

"That's what I'm clinging to."

"Exactly." He stared into space for a moment, then stirred. "Sorry, I guess I should go. You probably don't even feel as if you're getting a break."

"No, it's okay. I'm just sitting and chatting with a colleague. It's better than sitting in silence and staring at the walls."

"And thinking," he said, almost to himself.

Krissie forced herself to take a bite of her sandwich, chew and swallow. Ordinarily she loved tuna, but tonight it might as well have been sawdust.

"I'm just beginning to realize," she said, surprising even herself, "how much damage there's been."

"To yourself you mean?"

She nodded reluctantly, wondering why she had entrusted so much to a man she wasn't sure she should trust.

"I think," he said slowly, "that it comes to us a little at a time, because we can only handle so much mentally and emotionally. A little here, a little there, only as much as we can take at a time."

"It makes the process endless."

"I know." He sighed. "Better than a meltdown, I guess. And now I'll leave you to your meal. I need to catch a catnap." He rose and walked out of the break room, a tall, slender man surrounded by question marks and private demons.

Krissie forced down another bite of sandwich, and remembered something her father had been fond of saying: *You can go anywhere you want, but you always take yourself with you.*

Amen.

She put her head down on her arms and let the silent tears seep out between her eyelids.

Just as dawn began to fingerpaint the eastern sky in shades of red and rose, they lost another patient. A man, who had appeared to have no complications from the accident other than a broken leg and a cracked rib, went into cardiac arrest.

Krissie stood in the now-empty room, surrounded by the detritus of a code, and stared at the covered patient, fighting the strongest feeling that this shouldn't have happened. Unable to just walk away, she started wandering around, picking up scraps of sterile packaging, discarded gauze, used needles. She couldn't let go.

It wasn't right.

And then she saw it: the same doll that had been on Mrs. Alexander's bed only the night before. It lay half hidden under the patient's bed, probably shoved there during the fight for his life. At once, she picked it up at looked at it.

Ugly little thing, shoddily made. What the hell was it doing here?

A thought grabbed her, causing her to gasp. Then, clutching the doll, she ran out of the room and jogged to the nurses' station.

"Call Dr. Marcus," she told Julie. "Call him now and tell him to meet me in the break room."

Julie gaped at her but reached for the phone. The page was going out even before Krissie reached the break room.

As soon as she entered the empty room, she tossed the doll on the table, wanting to get it away from her. Her revulsion seemed extreme even to her, but she couldn't brush it away.

Standing with her arms tightly wrapped around herself, she stared at the doll and waited.

She didn't have long to wait. David practically

burst into the room despite looking as if he was drained of energy.

"What's wrong?" he demanded. "Julie said you seemed upset."

Wordlessly, Krissie pointed to the doll.

David walked over to it and bent for a closer look. "Wasn't that the doll Mrs. Alexander had? I don't understand."

Krissie licked her lips. "I found that doll under the bed of the patient who just died."

David straightened as if jerked upright by strings. "What?"

"Exactly. I saw it and…maybe I'm crazy, David. But why would Mrs. Alexander's doll be under the bed of another cardiac arrest patient? When I found it, I thought…I thought…" She couldn't even bring herself to say it.

"God," he whispered, catching her implication. "Is it the same doll?"

"I don't know. I just know it looks the same. As if somebody is leaving a message. David, we shouldn't have lost that patient tonight. He wasn't that badly hurt. And Mrs. Alexander was getting better. I don't like what I'm thinking."

"Neither do I." He looked at her, his dark eyes pinched.

Then she saw it, and backed up a step. "What are you thinking?" she demanded, horrified. "You can't possibly think *I* had anything to do with this. My God!"

"I don't know what I think," he said tautly. "I just know you've been here two nights, this damn doll shows up again tonight and you find it, and two patients have died. How would *you* put it together?"

Krissie shook her head and took another backward step. "No…no…"

He turned to the phone on the wall. "I'm calling the cops."

Cold and heat rolled through her in waves, and her vision narrowed. Weakly, she bent forward, hands on her knees to keep from fainting. The shock of what he was suggesting shook her to her core.

All of a sudden, strong hands gripped her shoulders. "Sit down," he said brusquely.

He pushed her into a chair and forced her shoulders down until her head was between her knees. "Breathe."

A cold sweat beaded on her brow even as the faintness began to pass. "I didn't…I couldn't…"

"Do yourself a favor," he said, his voice gentling. "Keep one of the others with you at all times."

A surge of relief washed through her, leaving her shaking. Cautiously, she raised her head.

"You don't think I…did anything?"

He squatted in front of her. "Honest to God, I don't know. I know how it looks, how it's going to look. But what *I* think…I don't know. My instinct says no. Hell, at this point we don't even know that anything *did* happen."

She nodded slowly. "Okay. Okay. Call the sheriff. Gage will know what we need to do."

Gage's arrival was low-key. Dressed in civvies, he came with Deputy Micah Parish and took over the hospital conference room. Krissie's relief had arrived to take over the day shift, so she was free to go talk to him.

She and David joined Gage and Micah at the long

table, coffee and the doll in front of them. Gage's scarred face regarded her impassively. Micah, on the other hand… well, the Cherokee lawman had long been like an uncle to her. His usually impassive face expressed kind encouragement.

Gage spoke. "So do we *know* we have a problem, or do we just suspect it?"

David motioned to Krissie. "At this point, she knows more than I do."

The two lawmen looked at her. "Go ahead," Gage prompted.

"Well, it was just one of those things that strike you. Yesterday, when Dr. Marcus and I made rounds, he found that doll—" she motioned to the one on the table "—or one very like it, in the bed with Mrs. Alexander. I thought maybe a family member had left it, but Dr. Marcus thought it best to remove it from the bed because we didn't know what might be in it."

"Possible allergens," David said.

Gage nodded understanding and scrawled something in his notebook.

"Anyway," Krissie said, "a few hours later, Mrs. Alexander went into cardiac arrest and we couldn't revive her."

Gage made a note and looked at David. "Was that highly unlikely?"

David gave a small shake of his head. "Actually, no. Mrs. Alexander was recovering from congestive heart failure that resulted from an arrhythmia caused by a prior myocardial infarction."

"English, please?"

"It was within the realm of possibility that she could suffer a cardiac arrest because her heart was diseased.

I wanted an autopsy, but her family refused. She'd been sick for a long time."

"So it's possible she died naturally."

"Yes," David agreed. "But I can't say for certain without autopsy results."

"Okay." Gage made a note. "I'll see what we can do about that. Then what happened?"

David looked at Krissie. "We lost another patient tonight, one from the auto accident. He wasn't that severely injured. Broken leg, a cracked rib. Prognosis was excellent, although there's always a possibility that he threw a clot as a result of his injuries."

Another scratch across paper. Gage looked at Krissie. "What do you think?"

"I was thinking pretty much the same thing. A clot probably. And then I saw that doll under the bed. It's just like the doll in Mrs. Alexander's bed."

"What happened to the first doll?"

"I have no idea. This could be the *same* doll for all I know. It's very similar, and I didn't look that close. But when I saw it, I was just so struck. What's the likelihood we'd lose two patients on successive nights from the same apparent cause and that that doll would be in their room?"

"Slim to none," Gage agreed. He tapped his pen on the table, thinking.

Finally Krissie could take the silence no longer. She hesitated and drew a deep breath. "One of the first thoughts I had was that maybe it's a message. Maybe these patients didn't die naturally. And Dr. Marcus pointed out that it looks very odd that I've been here only two nights, lost a patient both nights, and found the doll…"

She couldn't go on. Pressing her lips tightly together to hold back the urge to cry, she just stared out the window, waiting. Waiting.

Gage spoke. "Do you think that?"

David answered. "Gut instinct? No. But factually, if someone killed those patients, it doesn't look good, either."

Gage sighed. "No," he agreed, "it doesn't. And maybe that's precisely the point."

Krissie turned her head on a stiff neck and looked at him from eyes that burned. "What do you mean?"

"Well, if I were going to go around killing patients, I'd want to point the finger at someone else."

"True," David said. He almost leapt at the possibility. "I certainly wouldn't come to me with the doll and the suspicion."

Krissie spoke tensely. "You're assuming I'm sane."

"Aren't you?" Gage smiled faintly. "Okay, the first thing we want are autopsies on the two patients. They need to be carried out by a forensic pathologist, so I have to come up with a way of arranging that so we don't start a stir in the county."

Krissie understood that all too well. In Conard County, the grapevine worked at lightning speed.

David spoke. "Let's just say I requested an experienced pathologist. We don't have one here, and it would make sense that I'd want to transport these remains to another facility."

"Except," Gage reminded him, "Mrs. Alexander's family refused an autopsy."

"True." David rubbed his eyes.

"So," Gage continued, "we're sitting here with a suspicion, no foundation except a doll, and a lot of questions. I'll figure out a way. In the meantime, it looks like you both need to get some sleep, so get out of here and let me think."

Out in the parking lot, Krissie stood beside her car, letting the morning sun beat on her shoulders and ease the tension. She was wrong, she had to be wrong; that doll couldn't mean anything at all.

She only wished she could believe it.

Chapter 5

Krissie had the night off. It would have been so easy to call her parents and go over to visit them for the evening, totally avoiding the silence that made room for too many unhappy thoughts. She had no television yet to turn on for distraction, and reading was the last thing she felt like doing tonight.

Instead, she sat in her living room on a lawn chair as the impossibly long summer evening continued its slow waning. She'd slept and could sleep no more. She didn't want to think, but couldn't stop. She ought to make herself dinner, but couldn't rustle up the energy.

She despised herself when she got like this. She was a doer by nature, always busy, always involved. But periodically these dark moods would infect her, and the memories would start rolling, and she couldn't seem to do anything except give in.

A rap on her door startled her, causing her to jump. She wasn't expecting anyone, and hadn't been home long enough to have developed a drop-in-anytime circle of acquaintances.

Probably a salesman, she thought, and considered not answering. But finally, in the name of self-distraction, she went to the door.

To her amazement, David stood there holding a pizza. "I hope you're hungry," he said, "because I don't want to eat alone."

She stepped back, inviting him in.

"Sorry I didn't call first," he said, looking around her sparsely furnished place and finally realizing there was no place to put the hot pie except on the kitchen counter. "Uh…are you planning to hunt for some furniture, or do you just prefer minimalism?"

She gave him a wan smile. "I never had much, and what I had I left behind in Denver. I keep thinking I should take some time to go shopping."

"I highly recommend it." He opened the box, and wonderful aromas wafted out. "Plates?"

"Let me get them."

She pulled two out of a cupboard, then got two glasses and a couple of cans of cola from the fridge. They sat on her two lawn chairs at the battered card table she'd borrowed from her folks and ate tasty vegetarian pizza.

"I didn't get any pepperoni," he said, "because I wasn't sure if you ate red meat."

"I do sometimes. I've never followed any special diet."

"Would you if you could?"

After a moment, she shook her head. "I think not. I

find that I get too busy to pay attention to things like that, and I'd probably get a protein deficiency."

At that he laughed. "I hear you. The worst thing about being a medical professional is that you know what's good for you, but rarely have time to attend to it. And have you noticed how many of our staff go out to the courtyard to smoke?"

"It was epidemic when I was in the navy."

"Ditto for the army. I smoked for a while when I was a medic, then quit in medical school."

"It's the stress," she said. "Sometimes we relieve it in unhealthy ways."

"And in war," he added. "When you stop believing there'll be a tomorrow, who's going to worry about cancer?"

"Too true."

He fell silent a moment, then said, "I want to apologize for my initial reaction this morning when you showed me the doll."

She hesitated, at once relieved and uncertain. "Thanks, but are you sure you know me well enough?"

He gave her a charming, crooked smile. "I know, just two days. But yeah, I've been thinking about it all day. I've seen you in action, so I'm inclined to think that you genuinely care about your patients. So I'm sorry."

"No need," she said frankly. "You reached the first logical conclusion. I was stunned at first, but I've had a chance to reflect, too, and I probably would have reached that same conclusion right off the bat."

"Are you always capable of so much objectivity?"

"I doubt it." She managed a smile. "But sometimes it pays to think things through once your limbic system has settled down."

Another laugh from him. "Only a medical person would have phrased it that way."

Her smile grew more natural. Maybe he wasn't the kind of man she feared. It was just that her ex-boyfriend had been so controlling, yet so charming. The charm had kept her around entirely too long.

"So, about your furniture crisis," he said as he reached for a second slice of pizza. He flashed a smile that was both dark and disarmingly handsome.

"Crisis?" The word surprised her, then made her grin.

"Well, I suppose you could describe it some other way."

"It's not a crisis," she assured him. "I just spent too many years living out of a duffel, and then when I was in Denver I just never got around to decorating. I had a few things—a bed, a table, a second-hand sofa—but none of it was worth moving, that's all."

"It's a crisis," he decided. "If I were you, I'd ask my mom and sister to help me solve it. They both seem like the types who'd be glad to take you shopping."

Something, maybe it was an urge to test him, made her say, "What? You're not going to volunteer?"

He held up a hand. "If you saw my place, you'd realize I'm in no position to help anyone decorate."

"Ahh. So why are you complaining about mine?"

"I'm not complaining. It's just that I don't see how you can find it very relaxing. Every home needs at least one comfy chair, a good light to read by, and maybe a TV. Beyond that, I know nothing."

She laughed then, really laughed, and felt tons of tension seep away. "So your requirements are simple?"

"Actually, yes," he said. "The places we've been, the

things we've seen…I don't have to tell you how grateful it makes me just to have an easy chair and a decent
light to read by."

"I hear you." The darkness started nibbling again, but
she pushed it back. "Do you have any family in the
area?"

"Not a soul. What family I have lives in Florida—
my dad and two sisters and their families."

"Why did you come here, then?"

"Because somebody I met in a USO told me about
this wonderful place in Wyoming." His eyes twinkled.

Krissie felt herself smiling in response. "Who might
that have been?"

"Someone you know. Your brother, Seth Hardin, in
fact."

"Oh, wow! Did he tell you his story?"

David shook his head.

"Oh, man. My dad didn't even know about him until
he showed up one day on the doorstep fifteen years ago.
The details are Seth's and my parents', so I won't go
into them, but you could say that Seth was a blessed
event, even if he was already twenty-seven. Well, he
became a blessed event after my parents settled some
differences."

"I won't ask, but I'm dying to know. Seth's been re-
activated, hasn't he?"

"Yeah, unfortunately. It isn't enough anymore to
finish out your twenty."

"No, it's not." He sighed. "And here we go again. So
all right already. Do you ever lie awake wondering if
they'll call you up again?"

"Yeah." Krissie looked down. "I felt so guilty for resigning, but—oh, hell, David, I couldn't take it anymore!"

"I know. I know." He put down his pizza and reached across the table to cover her hand. "I know. I got the same way. I *feel* the same way."

Jumping up, she wrapped her arms around herself and started pacing the apartment. The pain inside her was nearly as big as the physical pain too many of her patients had been forced to endure. At times, she felt as if it would tear her apart. She could barely breathe, her chest was so tight, and a wire garrote seemed to have tightened around her throat. Oh, God!

Moments later, strong arms wrapped around her from behind, and she felt him rest his chin on her shoulder.

"I know," he murmured, rocking her gently. "I know. You don't have to be in a war zone to help people. Plenty of folks here need you too."

She turned within the circle of his arms, buried her face in his shoulder and started to cry. They were silent tears, but they wracked her body.

He held her and rubbed her back and said nothing at all.

Finally she hiccupped, "I didn't know I'd feel so guilty."

"Guilty for what?" he asked, voice rough with emotion. "Guilty because you gave all you had? Guilty because you were gutted and had nothing left? That's nothing to apologize for. Nothing."

She wished she believed it, but most of the time she feared that the gash in her heart would never heal. Or worse, that she might never be able to forgive herself.

It was David who got the bright idea. He called her sister Wendy, and within ten minutes she and her husband, Billy Joe Yuma, arrived bearing an absolutely sinful container full of homemade chocolate chip cookies.

"Oh, my God," Wendy said as she stepped into the apartment. "Krissie, you're kidding me."

"Kidding you about what?"

"Where's the furniture?"

David spoke. "We discussed that earlier."

"I haven't had time yet…"

"There's always time. You should have called me. We've got stuff we can spare until you find your own."

Krissie shook her head. "It's okay. I'm on my two-day break, so I figured I'd go shopping for a few things tomorrow."

"You need more than a few things."

They all settled on the living room floor cross-legged, in a circle with cookies and milk.

Billy Joe, or Yuma as he seemed to prefer to be called, was a war vet who'd flown medevac helicopters in Vietnam. He'd come home with some serious problems of his own, but had straightened himself out pretty well under Nate Tate's wing and with a job flying the county medevac helicopters. Wendy, who'd developed a crush on Yuma at a very early age, had gone off to become a nurse, working trauma in a big-city hospital until she felt ready to come home and take on the man and his demons. He was considerably older, but marriage to her seemed to have taken years off his age.

"Okay," David said just as the lingering evening began to dissolve into twilight, "we've got a couple of problems. Hence my distress call."

At that, both Wendy and Yuma perked up. "Hey," Wendy said, "I thought you were dying for our company."

"We are," David said. Krissie shot him a look but he

ignored her. "First of all, we both could use some
advice on dealing with demons. And then there's this
thing going on at the hospital."

Wendy scanned both their faces, then she said, "Sis,
don't you even have a lamp? I can barely see you."

Krissie went to her bedroom to retrieve her one light,
a torchiere. She carried it into the living room, plugged
it in and turned it on.

"That's better," Wendy said. "Okay, I presume we're
talking about the demons of war."

"You got it," David agreed as Krissie returned to the
circle and sat.

"Oh, that's easy," Yuma remarked. "Don't drink,
avoid drugs and live with it."

Wendy gave him a sour look. "That's it? That's
your best?"

He shrugged one shoulder. "That and time. I have
this theory."

"Let's hear it," David said.

"When you're all wrapped up in it, you don't have
time to assimilate what you're going through. The hits
just keep coming. But later, when you get away from
it, that's when you do your dealing. It's different for
everyone, of course, but you've got to deal with it, and
for most of us it happens once we get home. I don't
think you can truncate the process."

"I don't either," Krissie said quietly.

Wendy reached over and squeezed her hand. "We all
have nightmares, Krissie. Maybe not to the degree the
three of you do, but I've seen enough in emergency
rooms and as a flight nurse to haunt me."

"I know you have."

"Sometimes," Yuma said, "it just takes you over. You

have to let it roll. But you've also got to find a way to stop it when it gets to be too much. Some way to bring yourself back. Because the simple truth is that while you do have to deal with it psychologically, you can't let it take you over or you'll never be any earthly use again. My advice is to talk about it. I'm always available."

"Me, too," Wendy said. "And there's always a psychiatrist. But I don't have to tell you two that, you're medical professionals. You both know that these days they have some pretty good medications if it gets too hard to handle. Stuff that can help you get through it."

"I can handle it," Krissie said. "I've been handling it for a while."

"Me, too," David agreed. "We're just having a tough night tonight."

Yuma nodded. "They happen. So talk."

"Actually," David said, "for my part I think what happened today is kind of triggering it. Krissie?"

"Yeah, maybe. I guess. But I was having trouble before. That's why I take the night shifts."

Wendy nodded. "Go on."

"It's just easier to wake up from a nightmare to sunlight."

Yuma spoke. "Boy, do I understand that!"

"Me, too," Wendy said. "I understand. But the two of you strike me as functioning pretty well. So, however you're dealing, you're doing it."

"By working myself to death," David said. "But that's okay. One step at a time."

"The only way to go," Yuma agreed. "I got pretty well trashed for a few years, but you know that, Krissie. At least you're not doing that."

"Work seems like a better option."

Yuma smiled at her. "Trust me, it is. But what happened at the hospital?"

"We lost a couple of patients," Krissie answered. "But I don't know if we're allowed to discuss it."

David shrugged. "We weren't told to keep quiet."

Wendy leaned forward. "If there are two people in this county who *won't* gossip, it's the two of us. So what happened?"

David sketched it for them in quick broad strokes, including the fact that he'd called Gage. Wendy's eyes narrowed as she listened, and Yuma leaned in intently.

"Not good," he said.

"No," Wendy agreed. "It *does* sound suspicious. But why in the world would anyone do such a thing?"

"Why in the world," Yuma asked drily, "do people do such things all the time?"

Wendy looked at Krissie. "He can be a cynic sometimes."

"I wonder why?" Yuma asked the ceiling.

In spite of herself, Krissie giggled. "You two can be so funny." She looked at David and discovered he was smiling, too.

"But seriously," Wendy said, "it does sound suspicious. Without the dolls, I could just blow it off. Things happen, even under the best medical care. But the dolls are something else."

"That's what upset me," Krissie said. "I mean, yes, I was upset about losing the patient, but when I saw that doll everything went to a whole new level."

"Was the second patient in the same room as the first?"

Krissie shook her head. "So the doll had to have migrated somehow. Or it's a different doll. I don't know which one troubles me more."

"Either way is troublesome enough," Wendy agreed. "But if Gage is looking into it, maybe you should let go of it for now."

"Except for one thing," David said firmly. "I don't want her to be alone at the hospital. At all."

At that, Wendy stiffened. "Are you accusing her?"

"No, but the fact that this started her very first night puts her in the crosshairs any way you look at it. I'm just recommending an ounce of prevention."

"An alibi," Yuma corrected. "And I agree with you, David. If it turns out these deaths aren't natural, and if there's another one…" He turned his gaze on Krissie. "You don't want to be alone."

"But I can't always have someone at my elbow! Sometimes I actually take a break. You know, eat? Nap? It's a long shift."

"Then I'll cover you," David said firmly. "When you can't have your other nurses nearby, let me know."

"Oh, this is ridiculous," Krissie said. "It'll disrupt the whole wing. You're acting like this is directed at *me,* but I'm not the one who died. I wasn't even threatened."

David sighed, as if he didn't know how to argue. Surprisingly, that reassured Krissie—who'd been once again wondering if this guy wanted to control her every movement, even to making sure she was sleeping when she said she was sleeping—and her remembered frustrations and fears subsided a bit.

Just then, both Yuma's and Wendy's pagers sounded.

"Gotta go," Yuma said, as he scanned his pager.

"Me, too. Tomorrow, we go shopping," Wendy added, as she and Yuma headed for the door in a hurry.

"Do I need to go to the E.R?" David asked, checking his own pager even as he spoke. It wasn't sounding.

"We'll let you know," Wendy promised. She blew a kiss to Krissie, and they were gone.

Krissie stared at the nearly empty milk glasses and the carton of cookies on the floor in front of them. She didn't like this, she realized. There was absolutely no reason to think that anyone should be out to get *her*. So why was everyone acting as if someone was?

"I just got back in town a week ago," she said. "There's no reason anyone should want to get me into trouble."

"I'm not sure anyone does, Krissie. Hell, I'm not sure anyone has been hurt at all yet. It's just the configuration of the problem that's worrying me."

She looked at him. "The configuration?"

He gave an awkward smile. "I'm weird. I tend to see problems like vectors in a physics equation. What forces are pushing in what direction."

"Oh." She blinked.

"So I see a configuration here, a group of forces at work, and it's like they're all trying to point to you. *If* the deaths were suspicious. And in that case, you need to have some protection."

"I can't believe someone's trying to set me up."

"I don't want to believe it. But I keep seeing those vectors. And with the way things are configured now, if those two deaths weren't accidental, everyone's going to be looking at you first. And if someone's trying to set you up, there's going to be another death. And it's going to happen when you're alone."

"God!" She closed her eyes. "I have never in my life wanted so much for someone to be wrong."

"I feel the same way." He scooted closer and took her hand. "Try to think of it this way. If someone is out to frame you, and you're never alone, no one else will die."

She closed her eyes a moment, then nodded. "Okay. Okay, I can deal with it from that perspective."

She looked at him, and in an instant every other thought fled. He was so close, and he looked so good, and smelled so good, like soap and man. She had almost believed that she would never feel this yearning again, this yearning to be close to a man, to be held, to be touched.

Yet, as if someone had flipped a switch, her entire body wanted to lean toward David Marcus, to feel once again his arms around her, to find out whether his lips were soft or hard, to learn what the scratch of his cheek felt like against the softness of hers. To know whether the yearning she felt now could erupt into the maelstrom of passion.

His face seemed to move closer. Her breathing stopped, and her heart skipped a couple beats in anticipation. Some little voice in her head tried to get her attention, to remind her she was coming off a bad relationship and was anything but emotionally secure right now. But she didn't listen to that little voice because…

Because she needed to know. Now.

He didn't reach for her, but he bent closer, and finally, their lips touched. A brief, light touch that sent electric shocks running through her to her very center, filling her with heat and heaviness.

"You're so beautiful," he whispered, and kissed her lightly again.

More sizzles, more sparkles ran through her. Had she ever felt this way before? Not quite. Not quite like this or so quickly.

Danger. She didn't know him yet. Not well enough.

But before she could jerk back, he pulled away, placing space between them.

"Can I go shopping tomorrow with you?"

"Huh?" In an instant, every siren in her head went off. "You want to help me choose furniture?" she asked, a polite way of phrasing her real question.

"No," he said. "You can choose your own." Then he laughed. "I just want to spend a day with you. Get to know you better."

Not even her nagging fears could find a reason to object to that. "Sure," she answered, wishing every cell in her body weren't screaming at the sudden change of focus. But glad, too, because she had no doubt that if he'd kept on kissing her, she'd probably have made love to him right here and now.

And she didn't know anywhere near enough about him.

His pager went off then. Hers didn't. He glanced at the number. "I have to go to the hospital."

"Do you need me?"

"If I do, I'll call. Otherwise you stay here and rest. Sorry I can't help with the cleanup."

Another surprise from a man who kept surprising her. "Don't worry about it. Go. Go!"

He leaned forward quickly to drop a kiss on her cheek. "I'll see you tomorrow."

Then he was off, leaving her alone in an apartment that didn't feel quite as empty any more.

Despite all the lessons of her past, she nevertheless drew her knees up to her chin, wrapped her arms around them and smiled, savoring the memory of a couple of butterfly kisses.

Chapter 6

A relatively new furniture store had sprung up on the edge of town, thanks in part to the county's growth because of the semiconductor plant. It wasn't huge, but it had a sufficient selection and prices within reach since it didn't carry the big-name lines, but rather items for more limited budgets.

Krissie, Wendy and David met in the parking lot of Calendar's Furniture.

"Yuma begged off," Wendy said. "It's the despair of my marriage. He hates shopping." She looked at David. "What makes you different?"

He shrugged. "I need a few things too?"

Wendy laughed and Krissie grinned.

"Should we warn him?" Wendy asked Krissie.

"Warn me about what?"

"The Tate women," Krissie told him, "can turn

shopping into a safari of discovery. Be prepared. We are going to look at *everything*."

"Well, that'll be a change for me. If I can't stand it, I know where I'm parked."

Laughing, they went inside, but didn't get two feet before they were accosted by a woman who was about forty, with a bright smile and a trim figure, and hair that was beginning to show some gray—Jenni Lachs, someone the sisters had known all their lives.

"Hi, gals," she said warmly. "Hey, Krissie, it's been forever! Good to see you again."

"It's good to be home, Jenni."

"I'll bet it is. I never understood why people leave in the first place. What can I do for you?"

"We're browsing," Wendy said. "Can we just look around?"

"All you want. If there's anything you need to know, just give me a shout. I promise not to breathe over your shoulders."

Krissie's smile widened. "I appreciate that. I really do."

Jenni chuckled. "I don't like to make decisions when I feel pressured either. It always puts my back up and makes me want to say no."

The three of them wandered on toward the back of the store, away from the highest-priced items.

"So," Wendy asked, "what exactly are you thinking about buying, Kris?"

"Well, I'm actually happy with my air mattress for the moment. But it was kind of embarrassing yesterday not to be able to offer anyone a place to sit other than two lawn chairs."

"And I recognize that old card table of Mom's,"

Wendy added. "So you want to start with a dinette set? And maybe a chair or couch for the living room?"

"That's a good place," Krissie agreed.

"How's your budget?"

"Pretty healthy. I've had a lot of time to save and little enough to spend it on."

David spoke. "I need a table, too. I'm getting tired of eating at the counter or in my easy chair."

There were certainly enough tables to choose from. Everything from fancy to rock bottom. Krissie found herself drawn to a light oak table with an inlaid tile surface. The tiles pieced together a flute-playing Koko-pelli figure in dark green against a sandy-looking background.

"The trickster," Wendy remarked.

"I like it." She hunted for the price tag then winced. Wendy reached for it so she could look too.

"It's actually not that bad," Wendy said. "Especially when you consider you get real wood and that ceramic-tile surface. You won't have to worry about setting something hot on it."

"I know, but that's a big investment."

Wendy faced her. "Only if you think you're not going to use it for years."

That comment drew Krissie up short. Was she still thinking that way? Did she still feel as if the call was about to come at any minute, the way it had for so long when she was in the navy?

David spoke. "You know, Wendy, you just made me realize that's what I'm doing, thinking like a short-timer."

Krissie looked at him. "Me, too. That's probably why I hardly got any furniture when I was in Denver."

Wendy gave a little shake of her head. "We've got to get you both past that. You *are* planning to stay here, aren't you?"

"Yes," Krissie said firmly. David nodded.

"Then for heaven's sake, pick what you like, if you can afford it."

It proved to be surprisingly difficult for Krissie to do that, but with Wendy's urging she made herself. The tile-topped dining table with four matching chairs. A sofa bed that, the instant she sat on it, she knew she would love to curl up on and read. Or nap. And it was the same earthy green as the Kokopelli figure.

By the time she finished, she had also chosen a recliner, a TV and a stand for it, and a bookcase.

"That's enough," she finally said. "I'm going to have a panic attack if I keep this up."

Wendy regarded her sympathetically. "David seems to be having the same problem." She pointed and Krissie saw David hesitating among the less-expensive dinettes as if he couldn't make up his mind.

Krissie felt an upwelling of sympathy for him. She walked over and halted beside him. "Tough, huh?"

He nodded, then looked at her. "Do I want something cheap I can ditch later, or do I want to commit to something better? And while I'm standing here hesitating, I'm trying to argue myself out of that transitory feeling. I've been here over a year, after all, and I'm not having even vague thoughts of going elsewhere."

"I understand."

Their eyes met.

"I know you do," he said. "But you're doing better getting past it than I am."

"Probably because Wendy is twisting my arm."

He smiled at that. "So *you* twist *my* arm. What should I get?"

"I don't know your taste."

"I've never really had time to develop one."

"Well…" She hesitated. "Which ones do you like?"

He looked at the cheap dinette in front of him, then turned away from it. "That's just an excuse," he said. "An excuse to remain a transient. I actually like that one over there."

He pointed to a dining room table that could easily seat six or more. The wood was dark and nicely detailed.

"That's pretty," she agreed. "I like it too."

"Do you? Even though the wood is dark?"

"For a more formal table, that's the way I would go. I just couldn't put anything like that in my apartment. Do you have the space?"

"I have a house," he admitted. "One of the older Victorians on Front Street. I actually have a dining room."

"Then it would fit, wouldn't it?"

"Absolutely. In fact, it could even have an extra leaf in it and still fit just fine."

"So what are the arguments against it?"

"That I still don't have a kitchen table, which is where I'd probably eat most of the time, anyway."

"Hmm. What do you think of antiques?"

"I love them. Why do you ask?"

"Because there's an antique store out east on the state highway."

"I've seen it."

"You might be able to find an old wood table there for your kitchen." She watched him brighten.

"I like that idea. I like it a lot. Will you come out there with me after you order your stuff?"

So that's exactly what she did. She placed her order and paid and then was surprised to be told it would be delivered the following afternoon.

Then Wendy begged off the trip to the antique shop, because she needed to go on duty in a couple of hours. That left David and Krissie to make their own little caravan out the state highway to the Antiquery, as it called itself. There, in a cavernous barn, antiques and secondhand furniture mixed in disordered glee.

"Now this is for me," David said with satisfaction. "I used to love restoring old furniture."

"Yeah?" The idea intrigued Krissie. "I've never done it."

"It can be a lot of work, but it's the kind of work that fills time and distracts you. Leaves you tired and feeling good."

"Maybe I should try my hand."

"You're welcome to join me and see whether you like doing it. I don't know why I didn't think of this sooner. It's an alternative to working myself to death at the hospital."

"That would be a good thing."

They shared a look of perfect understanding, and Krissie once again felt that tug toward him. She had to make herself look away and remind herself that she didn't know him well enough to take such a risk.

Not that her body was listening.

David found a round table, about four feet in diameter that he judged to be sound, although it had apparently been painted numerous times. He picked at the paint with a thumbnail until he exposed the wood.

"My God, this looks like cherry," he said in amazement. "Who would paint wood like that?"

"Fashions change. Plus, maybe the surface is damaged."

"Maybe. But I can fix it."

She liked his confidence. She also like the appreciation he showed for wood. He hunted around until he'd found four chairs also made of cherry. None of them matched, but that wasn't as important as the wood, he told her.

"I agree. It'll add charm."

He checked the chairs carefully, determining that the joints were merely loose and the wood wasn't cracked, so they joined the table.

"That's it for now," he decided. "That's a couple of weeks of work. Then I'll come back for something else—maybe a chest of drawers."

He arranged for delivery, and then they stepped out into the warmth of a sunny summer day. The smile he gave her was boyish.

"I can't believe I didn't come out here before," he said.

"It's that permanence thing," she replied. She paused at the door of her car. "You know…"

"Yes?" he prompted finally.

"I'm just thinking it's weird that I'm feeling this way when I spent the first eighteen years of my life in a very permanent home. It's not like we even considered moving across town. Dad built an addition as the family grew, but we never talked about moving."

He leaned back against her car and folded his arms. "You were lucky to have that. At least you have a touchstone for what it's like to stay in one place."

"You don't?"

He shook his head. "My family might as well have

been gypsies. My dad's job took him all over the country, and I think the longest I ever spent in one place was three years."

"That must have been rough."

"I don't know. It was just the way it was. But here I am, determined to stay, I even managed to get over the hump of buying a house, and yet it's like living in a state of suspended animation."

She rested her hand on the roof of her car, thinking about it. "But I had a stable childhood and I still feel that way."

"Ahh, but you don't have a lifetime of it to overcome." One corner of his mouth lifted. "I can't even bring myself to hang a picture. That means putting a nail hole in a wall."

"Do you have pictures to hang?"

"I bought a few."

She grinned. "Then let's go hang them right now."

"Well, I've been excusing myself because I need to paint first."

She leaned toward him, lifting her eyebrows. "I sense resistance. What's it going to be? The paint store or hanging the pictures?"

"This afternoon?"

"That's what I meant."

"You're not pushy or anything."

She gave a laugh. "Let's put it this way—I *can't* paint my apartment. And I love to paint."

He pulled his keys out of his pocket and tossed them in the air once, catching them. "Decisions, decisions. Okay, paint store it is. Maybe you can give me some confidence in color choices."

"You're on!"

* * *

A couple of hours later, they arrived at his house with gallons of paint, brushes, rollers, drop cloths…everything necessary to get to work. Krissie helped David lug it all into his garage, a detached building that had seen better days, then she put her hands on her hips and looked around.

The exterior of the house had been recently painted and looked as neat as a pin.

"So you *have* been working around here," she observed.

"Not really. The place was freshly painted just before I bought it. Wait till you see the inside. That's where all the work needs doing."

They entered through the side door, through an empty mudroom, and directly into the kitchen. The appliances were all new, but that was the best she could say for the room. Too few cabinets, most of them old and battered, countertops that had long since seen better days, linoleum that was chipped and cracked.

"Did you buy a house or a project?" she asked him.

"A project. I had all kinds of plans."

"And?"

"Then I discovered that being here alone working wasn't enough. I needed more distraction."

Krissie nodded, understanding. "Well, I'll help you as much as you want. I could use some distraction, too."

"Thanks. That would make it fun."

"So, where do you want to start?"

"Right here, in this room." He walked over to a counter and ran his hand over it. "First the painting, I think. Once that's done, I can safely move on to the cabinetry and the flooring."

"Sounds like a plan. How is the rest of the house?"

"I'll show you."

He took her on the tour. Just as he had said, in his living room he had an easy chair, a good reading light and a TV, but nothing else. The old fireplace at one end looked as if it hadn't been used in years. "I need to get it inspected and cleaned, before I light a fire," he explained.

"You definitely do. Or maybe even closed off, depending on how much energy you want to conserve."

"I've debated that. Charm versus sense." He shrugged. "Maybe it's just a phony argument to keep me from doing anything."

She paused and looked at him. "We're a couple of messes."

"Sometimes."

The dining room was indeed big enough for the table he'd liked, but it was also wallpapered and some of the paper was peeling. "This is going to be a major job," he remarked.

The bathrooms had been modernized within recent memory, so they didn't require any immediate attention. There were three bedrooms upstairs, two empty and then his.

Krissie stood on the threshold, looking at his bed, a basic queen-sized bed with neither headboard nor footboard. An old chest of drawers stood against one wall, and the closet didn't have doors. Here, too, sagging wallpaper cried out for attention.

She spoke. "It's hard to believe this house got so little attention from the last owners."

"I have a theory about that."

She looked at him.

"People get used to things, especially when they happen slowly. Redecorating also takes a lot of money they probably didn't have."

"You sure have your hands full."

"I figure five years to whip this place into shape."

"If you get started."

He laughed. "If I get started. But you've kind of pushed me into that."

He glanced at his watch. "Well, we're not going to start today, anyway. I have to get to the hospital in a couple of hours. My turn for rounds."

Krissie's stomach sank as she realized that she was facing another evening by herself. But even as she felt herself sinking, she fought to stiffen her spine. Reality was that thing you had to deal with, like it or not.

David astonished her, reaching out to cup her cheek gently. At once, she caught her breath and felt that sizzle again. But his mind was on other things.

"I know it's hard, but it gets better," he said firmly. "I can promise, because I have fewer down times now than a year ago."

She nodded, and felt as if he'd torn part of her away when he dropped his hand. "Yeah," she said after a moment. "Yeah. See you tomorrow." Then she turned and walked out of the room, down the stairs and out to her car.

Sometimes, she thought, you had to face the devil alone.

David could see that Krissie left unhappy, but he didn't know what the hell to do about it. The simple fact was, they were racing too close too fast, clinging because they had a shared nightmare and not for any other good reason. He wanted desperately to help her, because despite his attacks of impatience, he had a helpful nature. Why else had he chosen medicine, with its many heartbreaks, as his life?

But he also knew himself, and knew that he was in no condition to really help Krissie. He couldn't even help himself.

Frustration, all too familiar, rose in him, and he toyed briefly with the idea of punching his fist through a wall. But he only toyed with the idea, because he'd long ago learned that you couldn't deal that way with the mental and emotional pressure cooker that war left in its wake. All you did was reinforce your own frustration and anger.

So instead, he climbed into the shower, forcing himself to move forward. Just keep moving, just keep thinking about the next thing and the next, because any other option would leave you curled in a corner in a padded room.

It had been a pretty good day, he reminded himself. They'd had fun, they'd thought about only good things, they'd both spent time making moves toward a more positive future.

The hot water beat on him, and he stood under the stinging spray, head bowed, telling himself that he could always call Krissie later and apologize for sending her on her way so abruptly. Or maybe not. Maybe it would just be best to leave her thinking he was some kind of crazy bastard.

Because, maybe, that's what he was. He saw how people tried to avoid him at the hospital. He was aware that he often had a short fuse over stupid little things. He was working on it, but the fuse was still too short.

Like the way he'd jumped all over Krissie the instant he first saw her, practically accusing her of malpractice in advance, for no better reason than that he'd made his own mistakes when he'd first returned to civilian practice. Projecting himself.

Bright, Marcus, he told himself. Really bright.

So, being a mensch, he'd apologized and tried to smooth it over, then—like an ass—he'd gone to her place, spent an evening with her and—stupidity of stupidities—he'd *kissed* her. Taking everything between them to a place he didn't think he was ready for. A place he was *sure* she wasn't ready for.

Damn!

The danger was that they might use each other as a crutch. Neither of them could afford that risk.

But his stupidity hadn't stopped with that kiss. No, genius Dr. Marcus had then invited Krissie into his life by discussing furniture with her, by showing her around his house, by asking her to help him paint the place and refinish a table.

Was he insane?

My God, whatever his own problems, he could clearly see that Krissie was fragile. There was something else there, something beyond the memories that haunted them both. Something he had seen a couple of times when she reacted to him, something that didn't come from Iraq.

He turned his face up to the spray, deciding that the best thing to do would be to return things between him and Krissie to a professional footing as fast as possible.

He didn't want to hurt her. And he didn't trust himself not to.

Chapter 7

Krissie's next two shifts were blessedly free of death and catastrophe. She began to relax into her new job and feel comfortable. She didn't see a whole lot of David, but he seemed to be busy elsewhere in the hospital. And she'd had an LPN as a shadow every moment she'd spent with a patient.

In a way it was a relief. So much had become so intense so fast, both at work and personally, and she was even having second thoughts about helping him paint his house. Not that she could justify backing out, not when she'd promised, but the idea of being in such close proximity to a man who attracted her while she was still scorched from her last relationship made her uneasy.

So the break had proved welcome, giving her some time to remind herself of her priorities and the distance to shake free of her attraction to David. And what an attraction it was. Maybe memory was a liar, but the attraction she felt toward David seemed to her to be stronger than anything she had ever felt before.

More than once, she had to batter down an urge to call him, to find out where he was, to get someone to talk about him. She was, she thought, in danger of acting as if she were having a high school crush. Time and again, she tried to remind herself that he had jumped all over her the instant they first met, with no better reason than that he thought he knew how she would act based on her previous jobs.

Somehow, though, reminding herself of this didn't seem to erase the more recent memories of a really nice guy.

She came off duty, after her second shift in a row, with gritty eyes and an aching desire to get home to her air mattress, only to be caught as she walked to the door by Micah Parish. This morning, he wore his deputy's uniform.

"Morning, Krissie," he said, his deep voice warm. For her, his dark eyes always seemed to smile. "Conference room."

At once, she tensed. "What's wrong?"

"Gage got some news he wants to share with you and David."

She tried to think positive thoughts, tried to believe that Gage was going to tell them to quit worrying, but she couldn't believe that.

Micah held the conference room door open for her and she entered, finding David and Gage already there.

"Morning, Krissie," Gage said. He didn't bother to smile. David nodded at her, but he looked as tense as she felt.

She took a seat across the table from David and nodded her thanks when Micah put a cup of coffee in front of her. Then Micah sat beside her, almost as if he wanted to be a bulwark.

"Okay," Gage said. He paused, sighed and shook his head. "I got the heads-up last night, but I waited until I received the faxed report from the forensic pathologist, because I figure you two know enough about medicine to understand what you're seeing." He shoved some papers toward David. "Basically, I gather that these two patients were murdered."

Krissie gasped. She looked at Gage, then Micah, as if hoping they were joking, but even as she did, she knew it was useless. These weren't men to joke about such a thing.

David hesitated, as if he didn't want to see the truth in black and white, then began to leaf through the papers.

"You understand right," he said finally. "These potassium levels are impossible."

"Potassium?" Krissie repeated. "You mean someone injected them?"

"With lethal levels," David said. He pushed the lab report over to her.

As she scanned the test results, a creeping sense of horror began to skitter faster and faster along her nerves. "Why?" she whispered, even though there was no answer. "Why?"

"There's another problem," Gage said. "Mrs. Alexander may have lived in this county all her life, but the other victim was from Iowa. As far as we know at this point, he had no ties around here at all. None."

Krissie slowly lifted her head and looked at him.

"It's random? It's random?" Somehow that made it even worse. "You mean this guy could pick just anyone and…and…" She couldn't even make herself say it.

"There's one link," Gage said. "The doll. We're having it examined, but so far, there doesn't seem to be anything about it that's threatening."

"Just its existence," Krissie muttered. Then she looked around at the three men, her face growing stiff and pinched. "And me," she said finally. "I'm the other factor in the equation."

Gage shook his head immediately. "I've known you for years. You're not the type."

"I wasn't the type. You don't know where I've been and how I might have changed."

"No," David said immediately. "I've seen you with your other patients. You care too much about life."

"And Ted Bundy worked with rape victims and escorted his coworkers to their cars after dark while he worked at the crisis center."

"Oh, crap," Micah said succinctly.

Krissie blinked at him.

"Crap," he repeated.

"I agree," Gage said. "Wholeheartedly. If you're linked to this in anyway, it's to frame you, and I can't figure out for the life of me why anyone would want to do that. You've been away for years."

Krissie didn't know how to respond. Their trust touched her more deeply than words could express. She ached. "Guys…"

Gage shook his head. "It'll take a lot more than this to make me even think about pointing a finger in your direction. The main point is, we've got a killer on our hands."

"Someone," David said, "who can apparently slip into hospital rooms with a syringe full of potassium solution."

"That could be a lot of people," Krissie remarked, struggling to maintain reason in the face of what felt like a one-two punch. God, two murders. Two real *murders*. Even though she had suspected it before, at some level she hadn't really believed it. Hadn't been able to believe it. Even with all she had seen of the world, she still couldn't imagine this kind of thing being real. How crazy was that?

"Exactly," David agreed. "Everyone from visitors to staff."

Gage pulled the papers back toward him and began to straighten them. "Okay, so fill me on how this works and what our bad guy would need."

David answered. "Potassium replaces sodium in the nerves. The sodium is essential for electrical conductivity. If you replace it with potassium, the nerves can't fire properly, hence the cardiac arrest. It's commonly used for lethal injection."

"Lovely," Gage said. "So anyone could find out about it?"

"It's not exactly a secret. It works fast and surely. When we get a normal potassium overdose, we can usually identify it quickly with symptoms and a BUN test, and treat it with sodium bicarb, which pushes the potassium into the cells and locks it up. But when you have a massive overdose, death is pretty quick."

"So, is it difficult to get?"

"You can buy it at the grocery store," Krissie said. "If you need to. It sells as a salt substitute. But there are lots of other places to get it. Dissolve it in water, put it into a syringe, inject it through the IV port so you don't leave a needle mark—" She shuddered with horror that someone could walk into a hospital room and do such a cold, heartless thing to a helpless patient. "It's too easy."

"I was afraid you'd say that."

David nodded. Krissie noted that his face had grown dark again, like the first time she had seen him. This had shaken him, too. "Syringes aren't exactly out of place in a hospital, either. You could walk around with one in your hand, and nobody would say a word."

"If you're on staff," Krissie amended. "Granny might be questioned if she showed up to visit with one in hand."

"And then she could claim she's diabetic."

Gage scratched his head impatiently. "Tell me something *good*. Something that will help."

"I'd suggest doing an inventory," David said, "except that if you're bent on murder, you can find syringes in bio-waste containers all over this hospital, and you're hardly going to care if they're contaminated. Then, potassium isn't a controlled substance, and it's one we have around for treating a number of things. We have potassium pills and IVs both. Not that it matters because, as Krissie said, there are a lot of places where you could get it."

"Are you telling me you think we have the perfect murder here?" Gage demanded.

"No," Krissie said. "We have the doll. It must mean something."

"One doll. I'm reliably informed that nothing the doll is made out of will hold a fingerprint. Okay, then, we need to be on our toes. Krissie, you need to have someone with you at all times."

"I already told her that," David said. "I have no idea if she listened to me."

She glared at him, suddenly wondering why she'd found him so attractive. The way he'd ignored her the last couple of days should be warning enough. "I've made sure to have an LPN with me at all times, but there's no reason to think anyone is after me."

"Maybe not. But if accusations come down the pike, I don't want to be the one to tell your father why I didn't make sure you were safe."

"Okay. Okay."

"We can pretty much assure she's not alone here at the hospital," David said. "Right now, that seems to be the important thing. I mean, if someone is trying to frame her by killing patients only when she's on duty, then the thing is to make sure she's with someone all the time. If it goes beyond that…" David shook his head. " I don't know. We're leaping at a conclusion here to begin with."

"Exactly," Krissie said, hating to agree with him but needing to. "It's a huge leap to think this maniac is trying to frame me."

"But it was the very first thought that crossed my mind," David reminded her. "Simply because you were new and basically unknown to me, and the deaths occurred on your first two shifts."

Micah spoke. An ordinarily silent man, when he had something to say, everyone listened, usually to their benefit. "While we're leaping to conclusions, there's another one inherent here."

Gage arched a brow. "That is?"

"That if someone has a grudge against Krissie, they may not stop at trying to frame her."

The conference room fell utterly silent as everyone tried to absorb that notion. Krissie stared blindly at the tabletop, her emotions so roiled now that she couldn't even tell what she felt, other than renewed horror. Gage finally spoke.

"Okay," he said. "Let's review. These patients have no relationship, except they were on the same ward on subsequent nights and that doll was found in both their rooms. The notion that Krissie might be the target of a frame, or worse, is based on the possibly irrelevant fact that the two murders occurred on her first two shifts. No murder occurred last night, right?"

"Or the night before," Krissie agreed. She tried to find hope in that, but somehow the darkness hovering around her didn't back off.

"Except," David argued, "you weren't alone at any time, were you?"

She hesitated, hating to have to admit she'd followed his directions, then shook her head. "No, I did what you said." But she immediately wanted him to know it wasn't just because he had told her to. "Because if this *is* somehow directed at me, I don't want to give the killer another opportunity."

"Now *that*," Gage said, "just raised my suspicions another notch. If this *isn't* related to Krissie in any way, why did nothing happen the last four nights? We need to check staffing schedules and find out if anyone who was working the nights of the murders was off the past four nights."

"I'll get on it," Micah said. "Might be good to check who else is a recent hire."

"Volunteers, too," David suggested. Then he glanced at his watch. "I have to run. I have an eight o'clock patient at the office." He hesitated, then asked, "Want to start stripping that table later this afternoon?"

He'd been avoiding her like the plague for the last couple of days, now this? Part of her wanted to tell him where to stuff that table, but another part of her spoke first. "Sure, if I can get my sleep."

"I'll call you around four. You're off tonight, right?"

She nodded, then watched him leave. Alone with Gage and Micah, she looked from one to the other. "I'm having trouble accepting that someone is out to get me. I've been away so long!"

"Some problems," Micah said, "follow us. You might want to think about whether someone from your past could have a grudge."

"Only my ex-boyfriend, and it's not like he could slip by me unnoticed."

"If someone is after you," Gage said, "it could be even more twisted than that. Your ex would probably come after you directly, not indirectly."

"I still think we're hanging a lot of suspicion on what just might be coincidence, in terms of the murders happening on my first two shifts."

"Maybe so," Gage said, rising. "But at the moment, it's the only thing we have approaching a clue, and I'm sure as hell not going to ignore something that might be a threat to you."

"I get it," she said, and rubbed her eyes. "An over-abundance of caution."

"Exactly. I'll follow you home to make sure you get into your apartment without any trouble. Micah, you dig around here."

"Consider it done."

Krissie gave Micah a hug, then allowed Gage to escort her to her car, much as it irritated her.

But that was the thing about living somewhere like this. Like it or not, the protective arms of love were wrapping around her. And given the way news moved in Conard County, Krissie had no doubt her dad had already told Gage and Micah to look after her.

Krissie awoke a little after three, surprised that she hadn't slept longer. As tired as she'd felt that morning, she'd been almost certain she would have slept more than seven hours.

Sitting up, she turned off her alarm, which she'd set for four in case David *did* call, then shuffled into her little kitchen to make coffee.

Laundry, she remembered as she rounded the corner. Her compact washer and dryer were in the closet at one end of her kitchen, and she'd dropped her knapsack there when she'd returned home this morning. Beside it lay the clothes she'd stripped off, too tired to even open the door and toss them on top of the machine.

Yawning, she started the coffeemaker, then went to get the hamper from her bedroom. Piece by piece, she sorted, throwing lights into the washer, setting darks aside for the next load. Then she lifted her knapsack to empty it of the remains from her supper, a couple of water bottles and—

The doll. *That* doll.

She reached out to grip the doorframe and stared at the ugly thing as shock hit her like a punch to the gut.

"Oh, my God!"

Her voice sounded thin to her own ears, yet still loud in the hush of her apartment.

The doll.

She dropped it as if it were on fire, and nearly tripped on her clothes in her rush for the phone.

Chapter 8

"Isn't this the point where you arrest me?" Krissie asked.

She sat on her new couch, arms wrapped tightly around herself, as Gage, Micah and a couple of other deputies went over her apartment with a fine-tooth comb. It was all she could do not to shake.

"Why would I do that?" Gage asked.

"Because that doll was in my knapsack!"

"Better yet, there was a loaded syringe stuffed inside it." Gage settled beside her on the couch, looking at her with concern. "Krissie, for heaven's sake, get a grip. I know finding it threw you for a loop. But just think. If you were responsible for that thing, would you have called me?"

"Maybe I'm smart. Maybe I'm diverting you."

"Yeah, right." He shook his head. "Calm down and think. You're in but not from me."

She had called David immediately after the police. Now he had arrived and was standing with his arms folded, leaning against the wall facing her. "One of two things is going on here, Krissie," he said. "Think about it. Which two things could this mean?"

"Other than that I'm killing my patients?" Her laugh was a little hysterical.

"Yeah, other than that," Gage said. "Either someone else was intended to find that in your bag during your shift, or someone is sending you a message. The thing I can't and won't buy is that you're a killer who is stupid enough to keep pointing the finger her own way."

"Or that you're a killer at all," David said.

She looked at him gratefully, but then shook her head, trying to drive away her own thoughts. What had already been ugly enough, and scary enough, had just climbed the scale to the top. And she was beginning to feel like the prisoner in the Kafka tale, unable to sort out any rhyme or reason for this new version of hell.

At that moment her father arrived. Even in his sixties, he managed to appear to her like the cavalry coming to the rescue. He didn't say a word, just bent over and hugged her tight.

It was almost as if someone had saved her brand new armchair for him: because it was empty, that's where he sat when he let go of her.

"Okay," he said, still the sheriff and always the dad, no matter how retired. "Krissie needs protection until we find a way to get to the bottom of this."

"I was just getting to that," Gage agreed.

"A four-by-six cell is probably the best way," Krissie said morosely.

"Krissie." Nate's tone chided her.

She looked at him. "Dad, if I were anybody else in the world, I'd be going out of here in handcuffs."

"Not likely," Gage said. "I saw your face when I got here. Everything else aside, you can't make yourself turn white as a sheet without a major shock."

"As a medical doctor," David said, "I have to agree with that. You're still looking too pale. And why the hell are you so busy arguing that you should be under suspicion? It wouldn't have anything to do with a little guilt about something else, would it?"

She glared at him, wondering how she could have been so stupid as to entrust him with that. Just like a man, to throw it back up in her face. "Don't psychoanalyze me."

David held up a hand as if to say *sorry.*

"Guilt about what?" Nate asked. Then, in a very obvious instant, understanding dawned. "Oh, hell."

Gage also seemed to understand. "I felt that way for years," he admitted. "All because I felt I'd failed. That won't work, Kris. It won't *help.* Not you, not your buddies, not anyone else."

Her jaw clenched tight. "Is everyone a shrink?" she asked between her teeth.

"Those of us who have been there," her dad said. "The war may change, but the price never does."

She knotted her hands together, remaining silent. What else could she say? The realization that they might be right left her without any protests.

"So," Nate said, "you come stay with me and your mother until we figure out how to get this guy."

"No," she said flatly.

"No? Are we that bad?"

She shook her head, and managed to roll her eyes

to make the point. "I just won't let him do that to me. I won't let him make me run home to mommy and daddy." It was probably a stupid stand, but she felt a desperate need to make one.

Nate smiled faintly. "There's my girl. So give me an alternative, short of putting Micah on your tail 24-7."

"I'll do it," David said.

She looked at him in astonishment. *The guy who'd scrupulously avoided her for the last few days was volunteering to be her housemate.* What's more, she wasn't sure she liked the idea of anyone just moving in on her. Her independence had been hard won. She summoned the only polite protest she could come up with. "You have to work!"

He shrugged. "I've worked so many hours in the last year, my partners had better not utter a single word of complaint. I'll take some time off and camp on your doorstep. Plus, I've had infantry training, so I won't be a useless bodyguard, and my presence here will just look like a hospital romance." He offered a little smile. "Much better sort of gossip than the kind that would come from having a deputy on your doorstep."

"And at work? I still have to go to work."

"Not for two more days," he said. "And by then we'll figure out how to handle it."

"Agreed," said Gage. "We're going to figure out how to catch this sucker by then or I'll eat your dad's hat."

"Eat your own," Nate retorted. "Took me years to get this one to fit just right."

In spite of herself, Krissie gave a little smile. Those warm arms of love were wrapping around her again, this time to distract her.

"Okay," she said finally. "But David, all I have is that stupid air mattress."

"I'll sleep on the couch."

"You're joking, right? *I* get the couch."

"At least I know where I rank."

"Yeah," said Nate. "On the floor. Do I need to have a fatherly word with you?"

David held up a hand. "Trust me, I know better than to mess around in your backyard."

Krissie wasn't sure she liked that at all. "I'm not anyone's backyard."

David looked at Nate. Nate looked at David. Then they both looked at her. "Yes, you are," they said in unison.

A deep laugh rolled out of Micah, and almost in spite of herself, Krissie smiled. Some of the tension was beginning to seep away thanks to all the support she was getting. Whatever was going on, she certainly wasn't facing it alone. And independence be damned, that was a good feeling.

David ran back to his house to pick up a few things he'd need at Krissie's, including his pillow. As he stuffed things into a suitcase, he wondered what had possessed him to make this offer.

But he knew. In his gut he knew. Something about the stand she was taking had touched him. Her refusal to be driven home to "mommy and daddy," while perhaps not the smartest move, had reached him at some deep level. She was fighting to hold her ground while forces she couldn't identify threatened her.

He respected that.

So okay, he'd just planted both feet back in the

middle of a situation he'd warned himself to avoid—
and with a woman he had very mixed reasons to
protect. Too bad. After finding out about that doll being
in her backpack, he didn't care about the other risks.
He just cared about helping to make sure Krissie didn't
get hurt by this creep.

After that, they'd just have to sort out anything else
that happened.

He figured they were both adult enough to do that.

Yeah.

Right.

Still shaking his head, he hurried out with his suitcase.

When he returned to Krissie's, all the cops were
gone except for Micah, who sat in his patrol car in the
parking lot. When Micah saw him, he nodded, then
pulled away. David went inside, tugged his suitcase up
to the second floor and knocked on Krissie's door.

She let him in, but didn't smile. All she said was,
"Hi."

He left his suitcase by the door, and watched as she
went to sit on the couch. She almost seemed to curl up
into herself, as if she were expecting another blow.

He didn't blame her for feeling that way. Finding
that doll in her backpack couldn't have failed to knock
her for a loop. All their speculation before that had
been just speculation based on what he called the "configuration." But now, it was speculation no longer.

He hesitated, not sure what, if anything, he could do
or say. Everything that popped into his head seemed to
be a pointless platitude.

Finally, he sat on the armchair facing her, because it

seemed stupid to stand by the door. Maybe she would say something, and give him a clue as to how he could help.

Seconds ticked by slowly, turning into minutes. Just as he began to think that he would have to do something, simply because his nature didn't allow him to sit and do nothing, Krissie spoke.

"I'm sorry," she said. "I'm being rude."

"You've had a shock."

She lifted her head and smiled wanly. "Yeah, but it's not the first one I've had, nor will it likely be the last. I don't usually go into a funk. I'm the kind who ordinarily gets a rush of adrenaline and drives everyone crazy trying to *do* something even when there's nothing I can do."

"I get like that, too. But honestly, Krissie, I don't know what we *can* do right now, except keep the guy from using you somehow."

"Yeah. Maybe that's why I'm so down. I don't like it when I can't see what's going on or why, mainly because I can't take care of anything."

"Nobody likes to feel powerless. But you're not. We're all getting together to sort this out, you included."

She nodded and sighed again, this time a more invigorated sigh. "You're right. And sitting here feeling sandbagged isn't doing me or anyone else any good. Maybe I'll bake."

"Bake?" David felt his interest perk about the way a dog's would when it heard the word "treat."

"Baking soothes me. If you don't mind, I'll go make cookies or something."

"I mind only if I'm not invited to sample them." That at least drew another smile.

"You can sample all you want."

She put him to work, too, which was fine. He wasn't a total tyro in the kitchen, he just didn't bother to bake. Once she had checked the contents of the cupboards, she announced they were making a chocolate cake.

"Chocolate," he said, "being the cure for all the world's ills."

"You got that right."

After the cake went into the oven, they returned to the living room. David, casting about for a safe subject, asked, "So what was it like growing up as the daughter of the sheriff?"

At that Krissie smiled. "Oh, I was very safe. Maybe too safe. Dad wasn't overprotective, he's not the type. But everyone knew who I was so I didn't have much room to mess up."

"Like being the preacher's kid."

"You're not the first one to make that comparison. Kind of like that, I guess, except that a preacher doesn't have the weight of the law behind him."

"So did you feel constricted?"

"Sad to say, I didn't often have the urge to do anything stupid. I had five older sisters keeping an eye on me, too."

"Is that why you left?"

"Sometimes I think so. I mean, a whole lot of things went into my decision, but yes, I think, like a lot of kids who grow up here, I felt a need to get away so I could stand on my own two feet. Spread my wings a bit. I always knew I'd come back, but I needed to make my own way all alone for a while."

"Glad you did?"

"Basically. I learned a lot about myself, and I guess

that was the point. What about you? How did you grow up?"

He shrugged one shoulder. "Very differently. Tampa's a big enough city to get away with stuff, and I got away with some. Nothing major, but I pushed the boundaries the way you do in high school. I got myself grounded more than once, I went to a few keggers I was too young for, I drove fast and picked up a few tickets, I ignored my curfew a number of times, and my dad threatened to make me drop out of school and get a job when my grades plunged."

"Wow. A real daredevil."

He laughed. "At times. I diverted most of my devil into dirt biking and girls. Much safer than some of the other stuff."

"But you enlisted right out of high school?"

He nodded. "I wasn't ready for college and I knew it. Graduating from high school felt like the end of a prison sentence, and I couldn't wait to get out and away. The last place I wanted to be was in another classroom."

"Funny, I didn't feel that way at all. I was eager to get to college."

"Everyone's different. When I look back at it now, though, I can laugh. I hated the thought of going to college back then, yet look at me now. I sure went back to school in a big way."

"You sure did."

He leaned forward, resting his elbows on his knees. "I think I needed a goal. When I got out of high school, I didn't have any idea what I wanted to do with my life. In that respect, choosing the army was the best thing I could have done. They gave me options I hadn't considered before, then pointed me toward medicine. That had never entered my mind before, but I'm damn glad I got here."

"I never wanted anything else. From the first time I can remember I wanted to be a nurse."

"Maybe because of Wendy?"

"Maybe in part. I have two other sisters who chose nursing, too, but one works in Casper and the other in Albuquerque."

"So they didn't come home."

"Not yet." She half smiled. "They will eventually. This place pulls you."

"I'm beginning to realize that myself. I sure wouldn't want to leave now."

She cocked her head. "So we both had fairly good, secure childhoods?"

He started to smile crookedly. "Which is probably why we both chose to turn ourselves into basket cases."

A laugh escaped her. "It looks that way. Except that's not true of everyone I met in uniform."

"Of course not. I'm just talking about the two of us. We emerged from high school with fairly intact psyches and then ran them as hard as we could over the speed bumps of life."

"So it seems." But she was still smiling. "There's probably a psychological message in that, but it's beyond me."

"I don't know that I would take it as a negative. I wanted to do something worthwhile, I just didn't know what it was. Something important. I suspect you felt the same impulses."

"I suppose I did."

"And no amount of imagination could have prepared

us for what we walked into. Not at first. I admit I came back for more after tasting it on the ground, but the Gulf War, bad as it was on occasion, didn't come close to what I saw in Iraq."

She nodded, listening.

"So I set myself up for the second round, because I wanted to be able to do more. Nobody to blame for that but me."

"We were already at war when I signed up," Krissie said quietly. "I felt it was my duty."

"I would have done the same, if I hadn't already been in."

"So there you have it. The tsunami was awful, but I was on a hospital ship and felt I was doing a lot of good for people. Then I got attached to the Marine Corps and everything changed."

"I know."

"I bet you do. It's not just the wounded, which was a nightmare in itself, it was the constant danger of attack from the unlikeliest places."

It was his turn to nod.

"You couldn't even feel safe on your cot at night." She drew a deep breath, clearly trying to shake it off before the memories moved in like an invading army of zombies.

Unfortunately, he was the one who got hit by the tidal wave of memory. All of a sudden, he was elsewhere, his nose full of the smell of cordite and burned flesh and blood, his ears full of the sound of men, women and children screaming and shouting. He was belly crawling through the dirt and over pavement—once again a medic instead of a doctor—because all he'd been doing was moving with a convoy to his new station when the roadside bomb exploded and the sniper fire started raining from the rooftops and the rocket-propelled grenades started to whoosh through the air, and he wanted to scream too, but people needed his help, and the bloody heaps of them were almost indistinguishable. Civilians or soldiers, men or women…only the kids stood out in their smallness.…

He had his emergency kit strapped over his shoulder, and he dragged it along the ground with him, ignoring the sniper fire because it was the only way he could hope to save any one of those people. He heard a soldier screaming "Ambush!" probably into a radio, he heard the sound of the convoy returning fire, but the screaming never stopped not even for an instant—

"David! David!"

He snapped back to Krissie's apartment in a flash. His heart hammered and he was gasping for air, and every muscle in his body had knotted up. "Sorry," he said raggedly. "Sorry."

"Don't ever be sorry for that," she said gently. She crouched in front of him, holding his upper arms. "Never, ever be sorry for that." Lifting one hand, she cupped his cheek. Her palm was soft and cool and so very different from the place he had just gone to in his mind. He closed his eyes and focused on controlling the adrenaline rush, on calming himself.

"It's okay. It happens to me, too. You know it does."

"It hasn't happened to me in a while. Not like that. I'm sorry."

"I already told you not to be sorry." Her voice was gently chiding. When he turned his face into her palm so he could inhale her scent rather than the manufactured ones in his brain, she didn't pull away.

Gradually the moment passed. Or at least as much as it could. Somewhere at the edges of his mind, the smells, the screams, the horror, remained lodged, a persistent background to the here and now. But it wasn't like a movie running in the background. No, a movie didn't *feel* like this. A movie couldn't make him *hurt* like this.

"Okay?" she asked after a few moments.

He nodded, his eyes still closed, and felt her leave him. For some reason, the loss of that contact felt almost as painful as the memories.

He opened his eyes, drinking in the evening sunlight, bringing himself steadily back from the precipice. "I had almost thought," he said apologetically, "that I was past that." This was his first flashback in at least six months and he couldn't have said which disturbed him more: the flashback itself or the fact that it had happened when he'd just begun to believe he might be done with them.

She had resumed her seat on the couch. "Maybe it's all this tension, and then us discussing it."

"Maybe. I hope I didn't upset you."

"Hardly. Been there, done that. I knew exactly what was happening. Want to tell me what you were remembering?"

He did and didn't. But he also knew that demons lost some of their power in the light of day. Talking about things could ease their hold on you.

"Not really, but I will anyway. I was coming back from a rotation home, on my way north from Basra to my new station, when we were ambushed. Roadside bomb, snipers on the rooftops, and too many civilians in the streets. I imagine you can fill in the details."

He could tell from her face that she didn't need anything more graphic from him to paint the picture. And that thought struck him as unbearably sad.

Lingering tendrils of overpowering memory kept trying to worm their way back into his mind. Not knowing what else to do about it, he rose and began to pace. As he approached the kitchen, the smell of baking chocolate reached his nostrils in full force, and it was as if a key turned in a lock. The memory withdrew fully.

"Hey," he said, "that's cool."

"What?"

"The smell of chocolate pulled me the rest of the way out of it." He turned to look at her. "Maybe I should carry a bottle of chocolate extract with me."

"What, and skip the joy of actually *eating* the stuff? Think of all the good things it does for you. And you can justify carrying a bag of dark chocolate bits around with you, because it elevates the mood and is good for the heart."

"That works."

"Better than tranquilizers."

"We need a new rule at the hospital. Every patient gets chocolate with every meal."

"Considering they serve enough sugar in the tapioca and gelatin the cafeteria is so fond of, they can't claim we're making our patients diabetic."

He smiled. "Works for me."

Just then, the oven timer dinged and Krissie went to take the cake out. As usual, she'd made it in a sheet pan rather than layers because she could use less icing.

"Do we need to do anything now?" David asked as he watched her put the pan on the cooling rack.

"Not yet. When it's cool, I'll make some icing for it."

"Can I lick the bowl?" He was trying too hard and he knew it. But he felt as if he somehow needed to make up for the flashback, even though she understood. Even though the flashback was not at all out of line with where he'd been and what he'd been through.

But maybe he felt embarrassed by it because he hadn't undergone anywhere near the level of trauma many of his patients had, either psychologically or physically. Now *that* was a stupid thought. It wasn't like there was some measuring stick.

"Do you," he asked suddenly, "ever feel guilty because what you experienced wasn't as bad as what others experienced but you still have nightmares anyway?"

"Now that's a good one."

He felt an urge to kick himself, because with just that one question, he'd put the shadows back in her eyes.

"Yes," she said finally, "I guess I do. In a way. I mean, I know I couldn't have done what those guys did. I couldn't have come back from a patrol with blood all over me, carrying some wounded buddy, and then gone out on another the very next day. Hell, I was having trouble dealing with the wounds and the occasional incoming rounds. But I didn't have to go *out there.* I can't imagine the places those guys had to go to inside themselves just to keep moving, to go on that next patrol, or ride with that next convoy. I can't imagine it. And it's not like they didn't have to deal with the same things I dealt with, too. And worse."

"I know."

"You probably do, since when you were a medic you went out on patrols. I didn't even do that."

"That's not what I meant." His own internal struggle gave way to a massive sympathy for her, and the conviction that she was beating herself up far more than she deserved.

"Krissie, let's stop this."

She turned her head sharply toward him. "What are you saying? Stop what? How do you stop this? Just the other day we were talking about how this is a process we just have to get through."

"That isn't what I meant."

"Then explain to me."

He hesitated, realizing this might be a case of being doctor and patient at the same time, and that he might be far off the mark. But she was making him realize some things about himself, and maybe those things were true about her, too.

"It just suddenly struck me that we're beating ourselves up when we didn't do anything wrong. At least I am, and you sound like it."

"As in?"

"As in feeling like we should have done more. That we somehow aren't entitled to our own scars because other people have worse ones. Damn it, we did everything that was asked of us. Maybe more than should be asked of any doctor or nurse. But we did what we were sent there to do, and that means we don't have to apologize for one damn thing."

She just looked at him.

"Think about it." He didn't know who he was imploring, himself or her or both of them. "Everyone over there gets their own piece of hell. Everyone. They may not be the same in detail, but they're still pieces of hell."

A shudder passed through her, and she wrapped her arms tightly around herself, closing her eyes. For long moments, she just stood there, unmoving. Then she looked at him again and said, "You're right."

A wave of relief passed through him, like a soft breeze on a hot summer day. She had just validated him in some way. He hoped he had validated her, too.

Impulsively, he opened his arms, and she walked into them. It was as if the sigh of relief completed as he felt her fragile body tucked close, as he ran his hands gently over her back and then embraced her.

For now, it was just enough to hold her.

Chapter 9

In the late morning, Nate came by Krissie's apartment. Because they were both used to working nights at the hospital and sleeping during the day, Krissie and David had stayed up into the wee hours watching movies and playing cards. They'd had only a few hours' sleep, and were still staggering around when he arrived.

Krissie noted with humor that her father took in the rumpled bedding on the new sofa and apparently decided everything was copacetic. She offered him coffee from the pot she had just brewed. He sat at her new table just as David emerged from the bedroom freshly showered and looking ready to take on anything that came his way. Krissie felt a good deal groggier.

She and David joined Nate at the table.

"Nice table," her father remarked. "Wendy mentioned you'd gotten one." He ran his palm over the tiles. "I like the Kokopelli."

Krissie arched a brow and looked at him from still-puffy eyes. "You didn't come all the way over here to see my new table."

A snort of laughter escaped David. He looked at Nate. "Does she always give you such a hard time?"

"From the day she was born. Hard to believe now I could hold her in the crook of one arm."

"I'm not even going to try to imagine that," David said, sipping his coffee. "We behaved, sheriff."

"I can see that. And that's not why I came. I hope Krissie knows that."

"I do, sort of."

"Sort of?" Nate raised both his brows.

"Well, you wouldn't say anything. You'd just *look* it."

Nate laughed. "You're grown up. None of my business anymore."

"So you say." But she had to smile. He returned the smile, making her realize just how much she had missed his warmth and that special father-daughter connection they'd always had.

"Anyway," Nate said, "I'm a man on a mission."

"How so?"

"Gage sent me."

Her stomach flipped over. "Why?"

"Because it's perfectly normal for a father to visit his daughter."

The ramifications of that ran around in her mind like rats seeking an escape route. "He thinks I'm being *watched?*" The thought sickened her.

"You know it's a possibility. You knew it last night when we didn't want you to be alone."

She did. She had. She wasn't a fool, but she'd been trying very hard to pretend she was. "Yeah, I know. I knew," she admitted. "I just don't like being reminded." And when had she become such a chicken? "I prefer to think that the point of keeping someone with me is to prevent that lunatic from killing anyone else."

"Well," Nate replied, "that was certainly part of the thinking. But we still have to look at the possibility that the doll in your bag wasn't just put there to implicate you."

She rested her forehead on her hands for a few seconds, then lifted her head and nodded. "I know. It may have been a threat. Sorry, Dad, for some reason I don't seem to be dealing very well with this."

"I can understand that, honey. I'm not sure anyone deals well with something like this."

"I've dealt with worse."

"You've dealt with *different,*" Nate argued.

"He's right," David offered. "Dealing with war, where you expect incoming rounds, is a whole different thing than the idea that you're someone's personal target. I don't know that I'd handle that very well."

"Or that any of us would," Nate agreed. "It's a whole different level, emotionally and psychologically."

"Okay, I'm excused for being shocked by what I already knew."

Nate reached out and patted her hand. "That's my girl."

She always loved it when he said that, and the way he said it. A genuine warm-fuzzy of approval. Lifting her cup, she drained half of her coffee, then said, "Okay, I'm waking up. Ready and willing to listen, because I assume you came to tell me something important."

"Gage basically wanted to know how you were doing—well, so did I—and he wanted me to tell you he has an idea how to draw this guy out. But for the moment, I don't know any details. Just that he's cooking up something, and given his DEA training, I expect it'll be good."

"He's set traps before?" David asked.

"More than one. Back when I initially hired him, it was as an investigator because of his background. He's really good at putting pieces together and making plans."

Krissie nodded. "I remember some of the cases."

"I'm sure you do." Nate looked at David. "There was a time when it was enough that I was ex-military. Then this county started going to hell in a handbasket."

Krissie giggled. "You always say that, Dad."

"I've been saying it for a few years now," he agreed. "Time was, we were pretty peaceful around here. Then something started to change. Damned if I know what it was. But crimes started getting bigger and uglier."

Krissie spoke. "Just don't blame it on the movies."

Nate smiled at that.

"Movies?" David asked.

"Oh, there was a spell when I wondered if people were being influenced by all the bad stuff in movies."

David nodded. "A lot of people have wondered that from time to time."

"I've even wondered on a few occasions if something got into the water. But the simple truth is, life here has changed. There's a lot more stress on people. Ranchers are having a hard time of it, and when they do, everyone in the county suffers. So it's kind of a roller-coaster ride. You can almost chart the crimes against the local economy."

"Wouldn't surprise me," David agreed.

"And of course, like any place else, we have our allotment of nut jobs." Nate grinned again. "I especially like our nut jobs."

"Why?" David asked.

"They keep us on your toes."

Krissie smiled. "You never seemed to enjoy it when it was happening."

"Of course not! I don't like it when folks get hurt. But you're gonna get the nut jobs regardless, and they keep us sharp."

She rose and went to get the coffeepot, bringing it back to top off all three mugs. "Any ideas on the nut job involved in this one?"

"Not yet." Nate sipped his coffee. "Damn, right now I hate being retired."

Krissie laid her hand on his forearm. "I know you do."

He sighed. "Okay. I'm supposed to tell you to go to work for your next shift. That's the day after tomorrow, right?"

"Right."

"Okay. He wanted to be clear on that. Other than that, though, he says to carry on as normal except for making sure someone is always within sight."

David spoke. "I'll make sure of that."

Nate gave him an approving nod. "You do that, son."

Krissie's thoughts followed an entirely different line. "It's going to be hard to act like nothing is going on."

"I'm not sure that's exactly what he meant. But I think he wants you to act like someone who doesn't think she's under suspicion."

"Why?"

Nate shrugged. "I dunno for sure, but I'd guess he's hoping to tick the guy off a bit."

Something inside Krissie formed an instant icicle of uneasiness. "What good will that do?"

"An annoyed perp often makes for a sloppy perp." Something around her father's eyes tightened. "Just be careful, honey. Don't be alone. Dammit, if I had my say, you wouldn't take a step without a swarm of deputies around you."

"I know." The part of her that hadn't iced over began to soften. "Oh, Dad, I know. But that won't work, will it?"

Nate reached for his hat and jammed it on his head. "I never said I was *always* smart. Most especially when it comes to my girls."

After her dad left, Krissie looked around, feeling at loose ends. "I guess I should make breakfast."

"Why don't we go to Maude's?" David suggested.

She eyed him. "Do you have a secret addiction to fat?"

"There's no secret about it," he said, widening his eyes in mock amazement. "And since I thought maybe you'd help me paint today, I think we can work off the ill effects of a slab of ham, some hash browns and a few eggs."

Krissie put her hands on her hips, ignoring the fact that they were still shaking a little. "Why do I think that's *not* really sound medical advice?"

He leaned close, saying, "Shh. Don't let anyone know. I'm not really a doctor. I just play one on TV."

They started painting in the living room, because it was one of the few rooms in the house that required no wallpaper stripping. David did the patching and spackling, so after a bit of sanding to make the patches smooth, they set to work with a coat of primer over the fading red paint.

"I love these old houses," Krissie remarked.

"They need a lot of work."

"And love," she added. "But you can see it's had a life. Look at these water stains over here. You have to wonder where they came from, because it doesn't look as if it dripped from the ceiling, and it's not near a window."

"Somebody got mad at a football game and tossed their drink."

"Really?"

He laughed. "Well, if you want to speculate about water stains I can make up stories for hours."

She shook her head at him, smiling, and went back to running her paint roller over the spot. "I'd prefer something more dramatic."

"Give me a suggestion."

"He didn't throw his glass because of a football game."

"No?"

"No, he was throwing it at the little gray alien who was coming for him."

David paused in his painting. "Now why didn't I think of that?"

"Because you've never been visited by little gray aliens."

"Ah. Have you?"

"Regularly. We have a scheduled poker game every month."

"That must be tough, considering they read minds."

"Is that why I always lose? I wondered."

"Duh."

"Well, don't treat me like I'm stupid. They never told me they could read minds."

David shook his head sadly. "*Everybody* knows they read minds."

"Not me. No one told me." She put her roller down and picked up a paintbrush to do the detail work down by the molding. "You ought to consider stripping this molding. Sometimes these old houses have beautiful oak or other hardwoods."

"I've been thinking about that."

"So I shouldn't prime it?"

He set his own roller down and came to squat beside her. "Maybe we should find out what's under that paint." He pulled out a pocket knife and used the blade's edge to scrape.

"Oh, God," Krissie said as the paint both chipped and curled. "That's *lead* paint!"

He muttered an oath and sat back on his haunches. "Well, hell's bells. God, I feel like an idiot."

"Why?"

"Old house, old paint? I should have thought of this."

"It's safe if we just paint over it, right?"

"People have obviously been doing that for a while." He rose, left the room, and returned with a flashlight. Squatting again, he pointed the light at the place he had scraped. Unlike newer paints, the lead paint curled a bit. It made for a sturdier paint, which is why at one time lead had been used.

"Hell," he said again. "So much for my do-it-yourself project. I'm going to have to hire someone to come in here and get rid of all the paint. And if I'm going to do that, I may as well have them strip the wallpaper, too."

She hesitated, looking down at the criminal substance. "I guess you can't leave it," she said finally. And there just wasn't any other solution.

"No. What if I have kids someday? And I wouldn't feel right selling the place in this condition."

"I can understand that. But I can't imagine the expense of having someone strip this house."

He grimaced. "I don't think I'm going to like it, but it's not as if I can't do it."

"I'm really sorry." Looking at him, she wished they hadn't made the discovery. But now that they had, he was right: he couldn't ignore it.

He rose, turning off the flashlight. "That's it," he said. "I guess we clean up the paint, then find out who to call. And once they start the cleanup, I'll have to find somewhere else to stay."

"You can stay with me," she said impulsively, then colored a bit at how eager she sounded. "I mean, you already are."

"True." He looked down at her, and his face gradually relaxed. "You have a very comfy couch."

"Wasn't I nice to put you there instead of the air mattress?"

"Absolutely. I mean, I like air mattresses too, but that couch is wonderful."

"So okay, where to stay is the least of your worries. Go start making calls while I carry this stuff into the mudroom to start cleaning."

He surprised her by stooping and brushing a quick, light kiss on her lips. "You're a gem," he said, then went hunting for his phone.

Krissie remained squatting for another minute or two, staring at the molding and grinning to herself. Those little kisses of his made her feel really, really good.

And she had just discovered the most profound respect for David Marcus.

She passed him in the kitchen as she began to carry roller pans, rollers and paint brushes into the mudroom. He was scanning the yellow pages, but around here there wasn't much to scan. Where was he going to find an experienced crew for this job? Probably from far, far away in another galaxy with the little gray men who were responsible for the water stains on the wall.

Her attempt at humor fell flat even to her. What was there to be amused about? David was facing an expensive home catastrophe, and *her* life had turned into somebody else's idea of cloak-and-dagger. It might make good fodder for a movie, at least the part involving her—because honestly she couldn't imagine a movie about dealing with lead paint, unless it was one of those old-fashioned government informational things she used to see sometimes in school—but it didn't make good fodder for a *life*.

She used the utility tub in the mudroom to begin washing the latex paint off the rollers and pans. Hot, soapy water did a good job with a little patience, and as she went, she cleaned the worst of the paint speckles off her forearms. The activity and the hot water soothed her, seeming to ease kinks from muscles she hadn't realized were kinked.

Some time later, David appeared with the two paint cans and set them on newspaper, where he hammered the lids back on.

"Any luck?" she asked.

"Actually, yeah. There's a local contractor, believe it or not."

She stopped washing and looked at him. "Surely, you jest."

"Frankly, I don't." He fell in with the old joke easily. "And don't call me surely."

"So who is this contractor?"

"A guy named Ted Gault, with County Contracting."

"Never heard of him."

"Why would you? He arrived since you left. Says he's been here about two years now, ever since they built the semiconductor plant. Anyway, he is a certified lead-abatement remodeler from when he worked for a firm in Denver. He was practically champing at the bit to take this on."

"Will wonders never cease? I thought for sure you'd have to look over a several-state area, and maybe wait weeks."

"Me, too. Anyway, Ted says he'll come out tomorrow and give me an estimate. He says it's not as bad as it sounds, the actual cleanup. They use heat to loosen most of it to avoid excessive dust. It's the disposal that's the headache, but he knows where he can take it. Regardless, nobody lives here once he starts."

"I'm glad you found him." She turned back to her cleaning job, and a moment later David was beside her, helping with the brushes.

"So am I. He sounds knowledgeable about it. Me, I never would have thought of using heat to loosen the paint."

"That's the last thing that would have occurred to

me. But then, there's all the wallpaper that needs to come off."

David shrugged. "Tomorrow we'll have all the answers." He paused. Then, "I'm glad you had me look at the baseboard. Honestly, I never even thought about it."

"It might have been perfectly safe. I mean, it was covered with later coats of paint. All sealed up."

"Yeah, but who knows what I would have run into when I started stripping the wallpaper? Some of that stuff looks like it's been up there since I was in diapers."

"At least."

Painting tools clean, they set them aside to dry, then looked at one another. David cleared his throat.

"I think," he said, "we both need showers and fresh clothes. Because you look as if you've been primed, and I suspect I do, too."

She looked him over, head to toe. "What did you do? Roll in it?"

"I'm a messy painter."

"Remind me never to let you near my brain with a scalpel."

"Hey, a scalpel is one thing, a paint roller is another."

"That's what they all say."

He leaned closer. "So how many doctors have you asked to leave your brain alone?"

All of a sudden, it became difficult to breathe. Paint, lead, handmade dolls and murdered patients took backseat to a strong urge to affirm life in one of the most elemental ways possible. But even as she felt the urge overwhelm her, David backed away.

"I'll run and shower," he said. "No point bringing these messy clothes over to your place. You didn't bring a change, did you?"

"No, I didn't even think about it."

"I didn't either." He spread his arms. "But this won't do. Make yourself at home inside. I'll be as fast as I can."

An errant, ridiculous urge to follow him right into the shower almost gained the upper hand, but on some level, she managed to retain enough sense to stop herself and settle for coffee in the kitchen.

Every time the man danced close, he danced away again as quickly as he could. She ought to be glad of that. After all, she was only a few months off a rocky relationship. She'd have to be insane to get involved again, wouldn't she?

But sitting in the kitchen by herself led her down even gloomier paths of thought, like the two murders at the hospital and the implicit threat involved in finding that horrid doll her in backpack. That doll had made it impossible for her to believe that people were leapfrogging to ridiculous conclusions. David's initial connection of her with the deaths had occurred to him only because they were her first two nights on duty, and to give him his due, he'd quickly dismissed the idea.

But that doll drew her smack into the middle of the mess. Two people had died, and while she'd had no hand in their deaths, that doll implicated her in some way, made it clear that, for some reason, someone wanted to hurt her, too, in some way.

It made her sick to her stomach to think that anyone could have cold-bloodedly killed two people just to get at her somehow. Whether this person wanted to kill her or just get her charged with the murders only seemed like a matter of degree when compared to what had already happened.

She lifted her cup with an unsteady hand and sipped coffee that had been heating just a little too long. Bitter. Like too much of life.

The one question nobody seemed to be asking was why she should be targeted this way. And it felt horrible to even be looking at it from that perspective when two innocent people lay dead. But it was the only hook on the whole thing: who wanted to get at Kristin Tate and why?

The boyfriend thing didn't wash. Al had his problems, but they didn't extend this far. The man was emotionally abusive, but he'd never laid an angry hand on her, nor even acted as if he might. His violence was more subtle and never of the kind that could have sent him to jail.

So it had to be someone else. And since she'd been away from the county for so long, she couldn't believe it was someone here with a grudge. So she must have brought something or someone with her from elsewhere. And there were a lot of other elsewheres.

She put her head in her hands, racking her brains, trying to figure out who she might have hurt or offended. But even as she sorted through places she preferred not to visit, things she would have preferred to forget forever, it came to her that a killer like this didn't have to be rational. He wouldn't need a reason. He could have just seen the arrival of someone new at the hospital as a good time to start his spree, because he could misdirect.

But how likely was that?

Pressing her head harder into her palms, she looked at things she didn't like to admit to herself. The young man dying of third-degree burns, with only hours left no matter what they did, begging her to kill him, to end it. She couldn't do that. But could she be absolutely certain she *hadn't* give him an additional dose of morphine? That in all the uproar and confusion she hadn't in some way overlooked procedure and neglected to record a dose so that she or someone else had given him a fatal injection?

No, she couldn't be sure. There were times when the patients came so fast and furious, times when the chaos went out of control, times when you forgot to log something, or forgot you'd done something, or maybe...

And this scared her most of all.

Maybe you deliberately forgot.

Dying patients were often eased on their way, quietly, with no ado. Never discussed. Never acknowledged. She knew it happened. She'd suspected it more than once, and had kept her mouth shut because when someone suffered that much, what help were you giving them by offering them another few hours of pain beyond description?

Or because in trying to help ease their suffering, you administered just a little too much painkiller?

The deepest, darkest gray area of medicine. Had she done it? She didn't know. Had some doctor given directions that did it? She didn't know. There was no way to know, because the greater the pain, the more tolerance a patient had to painkillers. Doses that would kill a healthy person often barely eased the pain of a burn victim or someone suffering from cancer.

All she knew was that she couldn't bear to think about it.

"Krissie? My God, what's going on? You look awful."

David came to sit beside her, and took her hand. He

smelled of soap, and some corner of her clung to the sanity of the scent. "Talk to me."

"I was just thinking…." She hesitated. The subject was taboo, but she needed to talk about it anyway, much as it made her heart ache, much as it terrified her. She cast about for a safe way of bringing it up.

Finally, she remembered something. "Do you recall that doctor in Miami a few years back who was charged with murder for giving a dying patient a morphine overdose?"

He nodded. "That put a real chill on pain relief."

"Yeah. Sometimes I hate to think of the amount of unnecessary suffering that has resulted from that."

He nodded and squeezed her hand gently.

"Anyway, if you recall the case, the patient died a few hours after being administered a huge dose of morphine. Apparently some nurse objected to the dose, so the doctor administered it."

"As I recall, yes."

"So there was a complaint to the prosecutor. I don't remember if the nurse made it, or if she told the family and the family made it. Although at that point, it was understood that the patient only had a few hours, maybe a few days at most, to live."

"Right. And the doctor was tried, but the case was dismissed after nationally recognized pain experts explained about pain levels, tolerance for drugs, and how that was *not* an extreme or even unusual dose of morphine for a patient in that condition."

"Exactly."

He waited, his gaze searching her face.

Krissie hesitated, then drew a long, shaky breath. "I was just wondering. I mean, I honestly don't *know.* But in all that chaos, what if I screwed up? What if I deliberately screwed up?"

"Are you trying to tell me that you did?"

"No. I'm trying to tell you that I don't know."

He hesitated, as if trying to organize what she was saying in his own thoughts. After a minute or so, he spoke slowly, carefully. "We can't always know."

"Why not?"

"Because when you have a patient at death's door, and you're doing your best to keep them from suffering the tortures of the damned, you're still dealing with an individual whose body might respond atypically. A patient who is *not* stable to begin with. A patient who could, literally, die from pain alone."

She drew another shaky breath. "That's true."

"Yes, it's true. It's an area where so many factors come into play, that unless you can honestly say you deliberately administered an overdose, you just have to let go of it or go insane."

She nodded, biting her lower lip.

"Look," he said, giving her hand another squeeze. "I had a patient four months ago. We thought it was appendicitis from the location of the pain, we administered morphine while we ran tests to find out what was going on. You know most cases resolve on their own, so there wasn't exactly a huge sense of urgency. The presentation was that she'd only been in pain for a couple of hours, which in ordinary circumstances would have given us plenty of time.

"Well, we almost lost her. The morphine depressed her respiration and blood pressure, then toxic shock added to the clinical mess because we hadn't realized that the appendix had *already* ruptured. It almost never happens so fast. So before we could clear the O.R. and get her into surgery, we had a nurse screaming in her face to hang on and stay awake. If she had died, we'd have been arguing about whether we gave her too much morphine which complicated the toxic shock or vice versa. As it turned out, she lived."

Krissie nodded.

"But my point is, when life gets that tenuous, with everything going out of control, with death imminent from other causes, you can't really point a finger unless you *know* you did something wrong."

"You're right." A short sigh escaped her as she thought over what he was saying.

"So," he asked, "what brought this on?"

"I was trying to figure out why someone would hate me so much. About the patients I've had for whom the most merciful thing would have been to ease them on their way because they were bound to die in a matter of hours anyway. And whether I had ever done such a thing."

"But you don't know."

"No. I don't." And she didn't dare ask if he ever had.

After a moment, he answered as if he could read the question on her face. "Before I would ever do such a thing, I would have to be damn sure I could live with it."

She nodded again. "I understand."

"Because any way I look at it, I'm not God. Pulling the plug on a patient who can no longer sustain life on his own, a patient who is brain dead, that's different. God pretty much made that decision already, and without machines, that patient would already be dead. But what I never let myself forget is that we're mere

mortals and we're not always right about when someone will die. So *if* I ever made that decision, I would
have to be utterly and completely convinced it was the
only right one."

"I agree." She closed her eyes, then popped them
right open again, because she kept seeing that one badly
burned soldier, the one where they could hardly find a
vein to insert an IV. The one the doctor said he was
going to put in a coma as soon as the line was going.
The one who went from screaming to death in a shock-
ingly short time.

"God!" She shook herself and jumped up. "The
memories!"

"I know."

He rose too, put their cups in the sink, and said,
"Let's get over to your place. Maybe stop and pick up
something for dinner later. The fresh air might help. We
gotta shake it off our heels."

"Yeah. Yeah, that would be good."

Because, while her mind kept trying to drag her
back, there was only one direction in which life allowed
you to move: forward.

"Do you mind going in the store on the way? Or do
you want to shower and change first?"

"I just look like someone who's been painting. Let's
hit the store. I need to keep moving for a while."

He nodded. He understood. And maybe that was the
best thing about David Marcus. He understood.

Chapter 10

David insisted on cooking. "As long as you're not possessive of your kitchen."

"Me? No way. Help yourself."

"My mother considered her kitchen to be sacred territory, and woe unto anyone else who attempted to cook in there."

She smiled wearily. "I wasn't raised that way. Far from it. With six daughters, my mother never had the kitchen to herself."

She left him to it while she went to shower and change. Some of the paint had dried on enough that she needed to scrub hard, but as a nurse she was used to using stiff brushes on her skin. This went a little further, but not much.

With her face turned into the spray, she thought over her conversation with David and realized he had skirted the issue of whether he had ever "eased" a patient over the line. Nor, she realized, would she blame him if he had. From other things he had said, though, she felt certain that if he had ever done such a thing, it would have been under only the most extraordinary circumstances.

And, God knew, there were times when she had wanted to, when it seemed like the only answer, the only thing she could do to help someone who was clearly dying.

When she emerged from the shower, the subject was still on her mind. She leaned against the counter, watching David season some chicken breasts. Waiting nearby on the counter were enough fresh veggies to make a memorable salad.

He looked up from sprinkling herbs. "You still look grim."

"I'm still thinking about our discussion earlier."

"About euthanasia?" He named it bluntly, using none of the euphemisms Krissie was used to hearing.

"Yes."

"And?"

"I'm thinking people outside the profession have no idea how hard it gets sometimes."

He nodded and turned to wash his hands. The two skinless breasts sat in an eight-inch glass baking dish, ready to go in as soon as the oven was hot. "Why would they, unless they've sat at a bedside with a loved one dying in agony?"

"True."

He grabbed a towel and faced her again. "This is really working on you. Any idea why?"

"I'm not sure. I mean, I was thinking about why

someone would want to target me like this, maybe make me appear to be a murderer, and for some reason, that subject popped to mind."

"But you said you've never consciously done such a thing."

"Right." She sighed heavily. "But what if someone thought I had?"

That arrested him. He stood motionless, then dropped the towel and pulled his cell phone off his belt.

"Who are you calling?" she asked.

"Gage. This could be important."

"I don't see how. Do you know how many people I've treated?"

He shook his head. "That's not the point. The point is how many people you've treated who have ties to this county."

That nearly froze her. She hadn't thought of that, even as she'd been turning the idea around in her head. All of a sudden, this didn't seem quite so Kafkaesque.

Needing to sit, she pulled out a chair from her new table. It would be perfect, she thought, at least in the mind of someone who wanted revenge. If someone out there thought she had euthanized a patient, and wanted to get even for something that couldn't be proved, what better way than to set her up as a murderer?

It made sense then. Horrifying, ugly sense.

"Gage? David Marcus. We might have an idea for you, but I don't want to discuss it on the phone." Pause. "Right, that'll be fine. We should just be finishing dinner."

He snapped his phone closed and faced her, just as the oven beeped to say it had finished pre-heating. "He'll be over around seven."

"I still don't see how this can be much help."

"Hey, you're the one who lived with a sheriff for most of your life. I'm just a doc."

"Well, it wasn't like Dad talked about work at home. I didn't exactly get a junior law enforcement course."

"So we'll let Gage figure out what to do with it. He's the investigator."

She helped David with the salad: washing, slicing and dicing beside him. It was a great time of year to make a salad, since most of the produce had been locally grown and thus perfectly ripened. One local rancher had invested in a hydroponic greenhouse to grow tomatoes most of the year, and the local supermarket gave them pride of place as soon as you stepped in the door.

And, as Krissie had noticed almost as soon as she returned to town, the local farmer's market had nearly trebled in size. With a troubled economy, folks with the land were making huge efforts to produce excess produce, and local folks were only too glad to snap it up at comparatively low prices.

"I'd like to go back to the farmer's market tomorrow," she said. "It's so different from when I left, and I'd like to explore it more."

"From what I hear, it's becoming a staple for local shopping, so yeah, I'd love to go back with you. I get lazy cooking for one."

"Who doesn't?"

Dinner proved to be mouthwateringly delicious. The herb chicken melted in the mouth and exploded with flavor, and balsamic vinaigrette made the salad flavors pop.

Krissie smiled at David. "You can cook for me any time."

"I may be doing a lot of that, depending on how long my house takes to clean up. And thanks again for offering to let me stay with you."

She waved a hand and smiled. "It's what neighbors and friends do."

They had finished eating and were loading the dishwasher when Gage arrived. He wore a chambray shirt and jeans and his trademark black cowboy hat. Not even when in uniform did he exchange it for the sheriff's tan Stetson.

Krissie offered him coffee and a slice of cake. He accepted both with a smile and settled at the now-cleared table with them.

"Okay, so what's going on?"

"Well, Krissie had a thought," David said. He looked at her, waiting for her to speak.

She had to admit that David never tried to control her, not even to the extent of speaking for her when he knew it was going to be difficult. It seemed as if her last resistance toward him was evaporating like smoke.

"Krissie?" Gage prodded.

She turned inward for a moment, seeking words. This had been difficult enough to discuss with another member of her profession, but now she had to discuss it with an outsider. But this was the man who had patiently played Monopoly with her when she was a young teen. The man who had joined her and her family for card games on Friday nights. The man her dad trusted completely.

"What if someone thinks I euthanized a patient?"

Gage grew very still. Then he drummed his fingers once, swiftly. "Did you?"

"Not consciously, no."

"But you think there might be a link?"

"I don't know." She shook her head. "I was sitting over at David's place having coffee while he showered after we painted a bit, and I was trying to think why anyone would want to involve me in something like this. I mean, apart from the obvious possibility that we have some lunatic running around who just happened to start his killing spree the night I started work."

Gage nodded, his expression revealing absolutely nothing. This man must have been something else when he was undercover with the DEA, she thought. She caught herself, recognizing her mind's attempt to deflect from the ugly business at hand.

"Anyway," she said, plunging into the icy water, "I was trying to think why anyone would have a grudge with me. And I started thinking of the patients I took care of while I was in the military. Horrendous cases, horrendous wounds. I can't even begin to describe…"

"You don't have to." Gage touched his scarred cheek, reminding her that he knew something of that by direct experience.

"So, all of a sudden, I was thinking about this one case. The poor guy didn't stand a chance. Severe burns over ninety-eight percent of his body. He was begging us to kill him all the while we were trying to find someplace to start an IV, so we could put him in a coma because he was suffering so much. And honestly, Gage, none of us thought he'd live long enough to transport. It was that bad."

"Go on."

"Anyway, I finally found a vein in his foot that had been protected enough by his boot…"

"Armor? The armor didn't protect him?"

"He wasn't wearing any. I don't know why. I don't know a damn thing about him except that he was the worst overall burn case I'd ever seen. Anyway, as soon as I got the line established, we pushed the meds to put him in a coma."

"Standard procedure with severe burns," David interpolated. "Pain alone can kill a patient, plus there can be massive tissue swelling, including the brain. With all the physical trauma already present, and all the very painful treatments a burn victim needs as soon as possible, medicine has moved toward putting severe cases into comas."

Gage nodded.

"He died soon after," Krissie said heavily. "It could have been shock from the burns, loss of fluids and electrolytes, maybe too much morphine while they were bringing him in, maybe the meds to put him in the coma. We'll never know for sure, and it really doesn't matter because there was absolutely no chance he'd have survived further transport. It was that bad."

"And this links how?"

"Well, it got me to thinking. Sometimes medical professionals…well, sometimes they speed a dying patient's passing. When the suffering is too great, when there's no possible hope."

"But you're saying that you didn't do that."

"Not consciously. I'm not aware of doing anything I shouldn't have, except that in those conditions, it's possible to slip up and make mistakes."

"But those are *mistakes*," Gage said. "We're all human, we all make them."

She nodded. "But what if someone thought I euthanized that patient? What if someone who was there thinks I did something wrong? Or passed word to family back home that I did something wrong? And it didn't have to be that patient in particular. There were so many." She closed her eyes, fighting back an unwanted urge to weep. But maybe she should just let the tears come. Maybe there was no limit to the tears that needed to be shed.

But instead, she blinked them back and looked at Gage. "So I just thought, well, if you wanted revenge for something that you thought was deliberate murder, whatever the circumstances, and you couldn't prove there had been a murder at all…"

Gage finished for her. "What better way than to set the perceived murderer up for some new murders?"

Krissie nodded and looked down at her hands. She had been twisting them together without realizing it, and now her fingers hurt. She kept twisting them anyway. Sometimes she felt she deserved to hurt.

Gage pondered for several minutes as he ate a few bites of cake and sipped coffee. "Thanks, Krissie."

"Thanks?"

"Well, you've just given me a possible motive for this madness, and much as I hate to say it, it makes perverted sense."

"But how does it help?"

"It helps me set the trap."

"In what way?"

"Well, if this guy wants to set you up as a murderer, and not as a victim, then maybe we need to start a little gossip going."

"Gossip?" Having been raised in a small gossipy town, the very thought made Krissie's heart sink. "My mother will kill you. I grew up hearing constantly that I mustn't give anyone anything to gossip about."

Gage half smiled. "I love this county," he said. "But look at it this way. With any luck, the gossip will only last a few days until we get the killer. Then I'll paint you as a hero."

"I don't need to be a hero. I just need my mom not to be on my case."

David chuckled at that. "I can sure understand that. Marge is a force to be reckoned with."

"Well, I'll reckon with her and your dad. Once I explain what I'm doing, they'll be okay."

"And just what are you doing?"

"I'm going to make this killer think he's just one step away from having you charged for murder."

Krissie didn't ask for details, and Gage didn't offer them. He was a tight-lipped man when it came to important things, and Krissie sometimes thought his wife, Miss Emma as she was known throughout the county, must have had her hands full getting him to open up.

He left a short while later, and once again, David began to clear the table, this time of dessert plates and coffee cups. Krissie started to help, but then just turned and walked into her bedroom, closing the door quietly behind her.

Once there, she made it as far as a folding chair before she collapsed and bent over. Every demon had its day, and today, more than one kept crashing through her gates.

Hugging herself, she rocked gently and let the huge, silent tears fall. They fell for the victims, they fell for the memories, they fell for every sacrificed life, and they fell for innocence lost forever. They fell for nightmares that wouldn't go away. They fell for wounds she could never heal, they fell from empathy, pain and even self-pity.

God, she loathed self-pity. But the memories wouldn't leave her alone, and the scars were still too fresh, and sometimes, just sometimes, she found it impossible to believe that her own mind could, or even should, mend.

The horror, the guilt, the second-guessing, the self-doubt, the loathing, the fear…all of it wanted its say and she had to let it, because sometimes she just couldn't stop it no matter how hard she tried.

She didn't hear David enter the room. The first knowledge of his presence came when he knelt before her and tried to wrap his arms around the tight ball of pain she had become. Somehow she unfolded enough to press her wet face into his shoulder, but she couldn't stop hugging herself to hug him back, because at that moment it felt as if the grip of her own arms was all that kept her from flying apart into a thousand pieces.

Her sobs gained voice, becoming noisy and ugly, wracking her. Dimly, she felt him twine his fingers in her short hair and gently caress her scalp while his other arm still held her tight.

And then eons later, she realized the top of her head had grown damp. Startled, she hiccupped another sob and leaned back just enough that she could see his face.

He was crying, too, she realized in wonder. Tears rolled down his cheeks, though he didn't sob. It was as if stone wept, yielding nothing except a salty rain. But it was all there in his eyes, the same consuming pain that devoured her at times.

Somehow that made it possible for her to let go of

herself and wrap her arms around him, too. They clung, tiny passengers on a frail boat being battered by a storm-tossed ocean, pieces and chunks falling away forever to the deep, dark depths of places no human should go. Places no human should survive.

Fatigue dried her tears and relaxed her body in the end. She sagged against him, and felt him steady her for a comforting few minutes. Then he eased away.

"Stay here," he said quietly.

She didn't even try to open her swollen eyes, just propped her elbows on her knees and wondered where that storm had surged from and whether those comforting arms of David's would ever return. Most men, she thought, would have probably headed for the hills at the outset.

Then she felt something cool and damp against her cheek. She pried open her eyes and realized he had a damp washcloth. He dabbed away her tears with amazing gentleness, then pressed the cool cloth to her eyes to ease their swelling.

"Sorry," she mumbled.

"No, don't say that. Sometimes it has to come out."

She didn't even try to answer. She was so tired, more tired than she'd been since they'd received an influx of wounded. Tired to the point that remembering even that could no longer shake her.

The dam had burst, and in its wake, her emotions felt like an arid, empty lake bed.

David dabbed at her face a few more times, then rose and disappeared into the bathroom. When he returned without the washcloth, he held out a hand.

"Come on, let's take a walk. It'll help."

The instant of resistance came from her past and she

knew it. Pushing it aside, she took his hand and rose. Even in her emotionally exhausted state, she felt the spark when flesh met flesh. It might as well have happened to someone else, though, because she had no energy to savor it…or even to fear it.

Dead inside. That's how she felt.

Twilight reigned and with it, cooler evening air, sapping the heat from the day. They strolled easily along tree-lined streets that played peekaboo with the view of the dark purple mountains in the west. Lights began to pop on in homes as they passed, suggesting cheerful warmth. She knew the physical reasons that walking was making her feel better, but she didn't bother to think about it. Instead, she allowed the steadily rising endorphins to lift her out of the depths, and gradually replace the emotional desert with a deeper sense of well-being.

Her step developed a spring and her pace quickened to something more normal for her. She began to notice the beauty of the old trees that arched over the streets and the way the leaves rustled in the quickening breeze.

"It's beautiful here," she announced.

He squeezed her hand. "It certainly is. Maybe one of these days we can hike up in the mountains."

"I used to do that all the time with a group of friends."

"I haven't exactly reserved the time for it since I got here, but I think about it a lot."

"I know some good trails I can show you." But she wasn't thinking about hiking trails. Where their hands met, an electricity seemed to be leaping into her, reminding her she was a woman with wants and needs. Steadily building an urgency she had not felt in a long time.

Virtually the last wall had fallen, she realized. Her heart skipped some beats, maybe out of trepidation, although she wasn't sure. It could just have been the rising sexual awareness that was steadily swamping her.

She could feel a heaviness growing at her center, and steadily filling her, cell by cell. Her ability to think about anything else faded in the face of her rising awareness of the man beside her. The emptiness she had felt such a short time before, that arid lake bed within herself, was rapidly turning into a swamp of desire, and like quicksand, it was dragging her in only one direction.

Her mind reminded her of how good she always felt when he touched her, reminded her of those light butterfly kisses, and made her want more, so much more.

But even that frightened her, because lovemaking with Al had been all about Al. His way, his desires, and if she got little out of it, he had accused her of being frigid.

She told herself she knew better than that, but the constant, repeated accusations had left her full of so many self-doubts.

So what the heck was she thinking?

But the heaviness persisted, and her entire universe kept narrowing to the man beside her. She was being driven by needs long unmet and maybe even by a need to prove Al wrong about her.

It was all so confusing!

Or at least she tried to tell herself so, because in point of fact, she wasn't feeling confused at all. She wanted one thing and one thing only: to make love with the man beside her, to find out if the sparks she kept feeling from him could explode into the kind of conflagration she had always dreamed of but had never experienced.

She realized suddenly that they had circled back to her apartment house. The urgency within her grew and almost without realizing it, she quickened her step. She sensed, rather than saw, David look at her in surprise, but he kept pace up the stairs, then stood patiently at her side while she fumbled with the lock.

Once inside, she closed the door, flipped the lock and faced him.

Then she did something she hadn't done in years.

"Kiss me," she ordered.

If he had a problem with aggressive women, it didn't show. He started smiling and closing the gap between them. "I thought you'd never ask," he said huskily.

"Ask?" It had been an order, but even that little quibble vanished as his mouth touched hers. Once again, it was the light, gentle, questing touch, but she wasn't having any of that. From somewhere deep inside, something more primal burst free. She grabbed the front of his shirt and pulled him against her, deepening the kiss with near desperation. What she needed from this man was something she was no longer sure she could get, but she was damn well sure she was going to try.

He gave her what she wanted, deepening and hardening the kiss, yet he never put his arms around her, almost as if he sensed what she *really* needed.

As if she even knew that herself.

Their tongues began the eternal duel, hot and

hungry, mimicking the ultimate act in a way that caused heat to pulse downward through her, building a throbbing at her center. A demanding throbbing, one that needed more, so much more. Erotic images began to swim through her mind, images of binding him so he couldn't escape, making him her slave. For once in her life, just knowing what it meant to *take* pleasure, the pleasure Al had always taken from *her.*

She started to pull at the buttons of his shirt. When he tried to help, she brushed his hands away.

"My way," she murmured against his mouth. She felt his hands fall to his sides. *Good.* Their mouths met again, hot and slick, sliding back and forth, even as tongues tangled. She was panting now, but the sound only added to her excitement.

At last she released the buttons and tugged his shirt down, pinning his arms at his sides in the sleeves. She tilted back just enough to take in the smooth, golden expanse of his chest, a chest that spoke of muscles well used, and a flat belly of the kind most men only dreamed about.

Gasping for air like a fish out of water, she ran her palms over him, loving the feel of skin on skin, delighting when she felt his small nipples pricked hard against her palms. Bending, she took one of his nipples in her mouth, sucking gently, listening to the gasp of pleasure escape him.

Her way.

She sucked his nipple to an even harder point, then bit it. Hard. He jerked and groaned, but she didn't let him escape. More bites, first one nipple then the other. With his arms pinned by his shirt, his only escape was to flee, and he didn't even try to as she added pain to pleasure, drawing more groans and quick jerks from him. Overwhelming him. Mastering him.

As shudders began to rip through him in steady waves, she reached for the buckle of his belt, releasing it easily enough. Then she began to push down on his jeans and boxers, wanting to work her way down his body and learn its every secret.

Now he was truly trapped, hampered by the jeans around his ankles, the shirt around his arms. Trapped as surely as if she had bound him. Even if he chose to fall to the floor, he was now truly her slave. The surge of power that rose in her was almost as great as the throbbing need that built and built between her thighs. Part of her listened for a protest, but it didn't come. She had reduced him to helplessness by dominating him with his own needs.

He let her. The most amazing thing was, he let her. He groaned her name when her hand closed around his stiff erection, when her fingers danced beneath and cupped him and found him perfect. She squeezed, teasing him with the threat of pain. He shuddered again, sucked air between his teeth, but offered not a word of protest. He had become her toy.

Her tongue and fingers danced over him, her nails dug into his buttocks, holding him still. She used her teeth on sensitive flesh until the groans that escaped him seemed to rise from his very depths. Until finally he couldn't take any more.

"Krissie, please…" The words were guttural, and she could feel him shaking now. Shaking for *her.*

Then, still fully clothed, she sat back on her heels and looked up at him. He stared down from sleepy eyes, his face a picture of need.

"My God," she murmured, "you're beautiful." And he was. Though his own clothes bound him like ropes, she could still see enough of his nakedness to know how absolutely perfect he was. She smiled, a very self-satisfied smile, because she had taken him to this point all by herself. By demanding he yield to her.

His answer was a sleepy smile, as if her words pleased him.

But he waited, still shaking with the weakness of need, letting her decide what, where, and how much. Power surged in her along with the desire that at once gave her strength and weakened her.

Reaching out, she pushed him to the floor on his back. His arms still locked in his shirt, his ankles still tangled in his jeans. Oh, she liked the way he looked, a helpless offering.

Standing, she faced him and began to remove her own clothes, secure in the fact that he could only watch and want. She had stripped for a man before, but never like this, never when she was in control.

Power fueled her desire like gas on a fire. With each piece of clothing she removed, she saw his gaze grow hotter. She took her time about it, too, running her hands over herself as she bared her flesh. Cupping her breasts and running her thumbs over her nipples. His eyes widened a bit as he watched, and he writhed in his restraints.

Her nerve endings sizzled like the fuses on firecrackers, sending signals throughout her, punching up her desire until it became a full-blown, hard ache between her thighs.

And just as she didn't think she could wait another second, she kicked away her own jeans. A long-buried imp took charge, and she straddled him, rubbing her bush over his chest, enjoying the way he watched her. She arched her back, giving him a full frontal view. Then he bucked up against her, as if he were trying to get closer to her. Oh, she liked that.

Desire hammering in her veins, she shifted forward and for just a few moments, brushed his face with her womanhood, feeling the enticing heat of his breath against her. She felt him struggle to kiss her there, but she was not ready for that. She pushed his head down, and continued to brush ever so lightly against him, teasing herself with sensations so fine they drove her even crazier with need.

"Just a sec," he whispered raggedly. "For heaven's sake…just a sec…let me…"

And finally she did. Off came his shirt. They struggled together with his jeans and boots, but just as she was about to mount him again, he defied her. She knew a moment of consternation, but forced herself to wait.

It was almost too long as he pawed in his pants, but when he drew out a condom, she understood. She grabbed the packet from him, ripped it open, then rolled it onto his member, taking her time, loving the way he groaned at each touch. "Smart man," she whispered, running her fingers over the latex and watching his member jump in response.

He was so ready. But so was she.

Then she pushed him back by his shoulders and rose over him, straddling him.

Her way.

He reached down, guiding himself, and then she caught her breath and slowly, slowly, she filled the aching need in herself, filling a place too long empty, feeling

the ripples of pleasure spread outward, needing…
needing…needing…

She gasped and threw back her head, when she
settled fully on him. Her eyes opened a crack and found
him looking up at her with the same hunger, the same
wonder, the same incredible need.

Leaning forward so as not to hurt him, she braced
her palms on the floor beside his shoulders and began
to move, pressing herself to him in just the way *she*
needed, his gasps blending with hers, his groans joining
hers as the pace quickened, and the hunger grew, as the
fuses along every nerve ending sizzled.

And then it happened. In one incredible moment, in
a universe that existed only between lovers, she
exploded into a supernova of completion. But the
pulsing didn't stop, it went on, driving her into another
explosion, and another…

Until the universe went black and she collapsed.

Chapter 11

David pulled the comforter from the air mattress and wrapped them cozily in it as they lay on the living room floor.

For a long, long time they cuddled close, just content to be. Their lovemaking had created a cocoon that locked everything else out, and neither of them seemed in any hurry to disturb it.

Idly, from time to time, their hands traced one another's bodies. There was nothing like the sense of freedom that came from being able to lie naked like this with someone, with nothing left to hide, at least in this arena. Yearnings that had been silent, and had held an element of fear, especially fear of rejection, were now out in the open.

It felt wonderful.

It felt even more wonderful to Krissie to realize that

she had crossed a major hurdle and had just thrown Al permanently and finally into the trash heap of the past.

David had allowed her to take control. And while she suspected that wouldn't always be the case, she didn't need it to be. It was enough, quite enough, that he could relinquish control when she needed it.

"God," she said suddenly, quietly.

"Hmm?" he asked, nuzzling her neck.

"I was just thinking. I blew through a couple of major emotional blocks today. I should either be celebrating or dying of exhaustion."

A quiet chuckle escaped him. "We can go get champagne if you like."

She liked that he didn't question her about it, didn't demand an explanation. He was willing to give her room to talk when she was ready.

Come to think of it, David Marcus was a pretty special guy.

If she dared to trust her own judgment, that was, and right now she felt she could.

"No champagne," she said, turning into him, bringing their bodies even closer. "There are plenty of other ways to celebrate."

"Not until I get another condom," he replied, opening one eye. "I don't exactly carry a box of them with me."

"Then maybe you should get inventive."

She watched the slow smile creep across his face. "Are you challenging me?"

"Depends on how you want to take it."

Another laugh escaped him. "Oh, sweetie, I can get creative. I can get *really* creative."

"Then show me!"

He did.

At first he had her giggling and squirming as he teased her with his tongue, trailing it across sensitive places like the inside of her upper arms.

"Hey," she said between giggles at one point, "didn't anyone ever tell you that the quickest way to kill the mood is with laughter?"

"Depends on what you're laughing about."

And he was so, so right. Gasping giggles gave way to plain gasps, and she stopped wiggling away from those ticklish touches to wiggling closer to them, wanting even more.

He seemed to be painting fire over every inch of her, little embers that glowed and grew brighter and began to shoot off sparks. By the time he reached her nipples, she was so aroused she could barely stand it when he ran his tongue in damp rings around them, but refused to touch them. Finally, in desperation, she reached out and pulled his head closer, guiding him to one nipple.

That seemed to please him as much as her, for a guttural sound escaped him as he latched on and began to suck powerfully in a rhythm that was soon echoed by her entire body, a rhythm that sent pulses of heat to her very center, causing her to cross her legs tightly, trying to find the pressure she needed down there, too....

She left her mind behind, and she didn't care. This was mindlessness at its best, and for now, right now, nothing existed except exquisite sensation, exquisite hunger.

More!

He settled between her legs, his tongue tracing patterns on her labia, avoiding the sensitive nub that was once again aching, until her hips bucked and rotated in a search for even deeper touches, stronger touches. He was a tease, though, and in the process taught her she had hyper-sensitive places she had never before discovered. Lower he went, past the place he had shared with her only a short while before, nearing a place she had never shared with anyone, still teasing, until she cried out.

Then back he came, slowly, promising but never giving, holding her thrall as surely as if she were the one bound now. Circling, drawing gasps from her as she tried to bring herself into exactly the right position where he could no longer deny her the touches she hungered for. His tongue dipped into her, again and again, but it still wasn't enough.

Then, just as she thought the anticipation would kill her, he gave her what she needed. He took the exquisitely bundled nerve endings into his mouth, and nipped, sending shockwaves of heat through her. Only when she cried out again did he begin to lick her in that irresistible rhythm.

Only this time wasn't a few paltry bottle rockets. No, she got the whole damn fireworks show, start to finish, explosion after explosion of heat and light.

Wrapped finally in his arms, she never wanted to move again.

Later, hungry, they made a small plate of crackers and cheese and curled up on the couch together. She wore an outsize blue T-shirt that she had owned for so many years it was on the verge of becoming see-through. He donned a white T-shirt and boxers. They kept the comforter close, kind of piled around them like a nest, and nibbled at the food while soft music played in the background.

Mostly they talked. She recalled fishing trips with her dad, including one where he swore he was going to lose his mind if all six girls didn't stop running in different directions in the woods. She told him about the time he'd tried to teach them to fly-cast and had wound up hooking a bird in flight.

"Can you imagine it?" she said with a smile. "My poor dad. He was as distressed as any of us, I'm sure, and had to reel the poor thing in while it was flapping like mad to escape, and he had all of us standing around shrieking at him to save the bird, that he'd killed it, that we were never going fishing again. Somebody, I don't remember who, even told him she would never speak to him again if that bird died."

"Ouch." He feigned a wince, but there was a smile in his eyes.

"Dad got the bird off the hook, though, and it flew away. There didn't seem to be much blood, so I guess it didn't suffer much damage."

"Did you go fly fishing after that?"

Krissie shook her head. "Never. Dad never even suggested it. After that it was all about standing on the creek bank dragging bait on a bobber. That was good enough for me, though. We always caught enough for breakfast or supper, depending, and nothing tasted better than those fish right out of the water, cooked over an open fire."

"I used to love that, too, although I doubt I went fishing as often as you did. But I've got a story just as good."

"Yeah?" She looked at him expectantly.

"Yeah. We were on a camping trip somewhere. Odd that I don't even remember where." He knit his brow. "Oh, well. We used to have one of those pop-up campers, a step up from a tent. Anyway, I was maybe four or five, and I can remember sitting in the dirt and pine needles making roads for my Matchbox cars. I never traveled without them."

"Really?" She smiled. "That's cute."

"Don't tell anyone, but I still have them all. You could say I was very much attached to them. Anyway, there I was involved in the very important business of building superhighways complete with pine-needle berms when my dad called to me. I turned my head, and he was holding this small snake for me to see."

"Oh, my gosh!"

"That was my mother's reaction. She started screaming at him, telling him to put it down, it was a snake. And he said, 'It's just a garter snake. It won't hurt me.' At that exact moment, it bit him."

"Oh, no!" Krissie couldn't help laughing. "You're kidding!"

He held up his right hand. "Scout's honor. I can still remember the two holes in his thumb. And my mother still screaming what was he thinking of, teaching us kids to pick up snakes. The funny thing was, after seeing that, I never again had any desire whatsoever to pick up a snake. Even a small garter snake. Lesson learned, despite what my mother thought."

Krissie was still chuckling. "I can understand her point though."

"Of course. She wasn't mad at him, though. I can still remember her tone. She was screaming because she was scared."

"Well, of course, if she didn't know much about snakes. And I can sure see why she thought he was setting a bad example for you."

"Yup." David's smile broadened. "Afterward, he leaned close and said, 'Sonny, that's why you should never fool around with wild creatures.'"

"Sounds like a big man."

"He *is* a big man, despite being in his eighties. His heart was always in a good place."

"So he called you Sonny?"

"Until I got older and wouldn't stand for it. Sometimes now I miss it, though."

She nodded and leaned her head on his shoulder, reveling in the newfound freedom to be able to do that. "I was always Krissie to everyone, except once in a while Kris. When someone called me Kristin, I knew I was in deep trouble."

He laughed at that. "Did you get the middle name thing, too?"

"Of course. I think it must be in the parent genes. Kristin Elizabeth. I'd hear that and want to find a deep dark hole to hide in."

She could feel him nod against the top of her head. "For me it was David Andrew. You want to shut me up in an instant, called me David Andrew."

"Dad can still silence me with that."

"Same here. Although I have to admit it's been a long while since he felt the urge."

She nuzzled his shoulder a bit, inhaling deep drafts of his scent. Never had another human being smelled quite so good to her. "How do they feel about you choosing to live all the way up here?"

"They're okay with it. According to my mom,

they're just grateful they don't have to worry about me all day every day."

"That has to be so important to them."

He kissed the top of her head. "I think families have a harder time of it in some ways."

"In terms of worry, most certainly."

He was silent for a moment, then, "Did your dad try to talk you out of signing up?"

"Yes. Once. He only tried once."

"What did he say?"

"That he understood why I wanted to do it, that maybe he'd raised me with too strong a sense of duty. And finally, that there was no way I could begin to understand what I was walking into."

"Which of course was true."

"He was absolutely right about that." She stirred a little, sighing. "But he didn't exactly try to change my mind. It's hard to explain. I think mostly he wanted me to think it through hard before I took the step, but once my mind was made up, all he said was that he was damn proud of me. It was almost as if he felt I was doing the right thing, but as a parent he was scared for me, if that makes sense."

"It makes perfect sense, especially given that we were already at war. That wasn't an issue for my family when I first enlisted. You could almost hear the marching bands in the background. They threw a party, my dad told me he was proud that I was stepping up to be a man, and serve my country. The tune didn't change until I re-upped after the Gulf War. Then I heard about how I'd done my bit and I could be a civilian doctor just as well. But by then, I'd seen the very things that made me want to go to medical school and there was no way I was going to quit."

She shook her head a little. "In the end we both had to get out."

"But it wasn't *quitting*," he said firmly. "Don't you start feeling guilty again. If they needed either of us, we'd be back there right now."

"You're right." She hadn't thought of it that way, and in her heart, a little flame of light appeared. "Yeah, you're right." She sat up. "They recall anyone they need, like my brother. The fact that they let us go—"

"—means we aren't essential. For whatever reason, they've got enough medical people."

She looked at him and smiled. "Thank you for that. I really didn't see it that way."

"I know you didn't. But unlike the boots on the ground, we don't seem to be irreplaceable. So hallelujah for that, because I'm not sure I wouldn't have blown a gasket."

He leaned toward her. "You know the one thing nobody talks about?"

"What's that?"

"That the troops get to vent their rage and anger when they get into a bad situation. They get to fight back. You and me? We see the results of it all, we get angry, and we can't afford to let it out. We have to bottle it in every single minute of the day. Hell, they don't even let us pick up a gun and go shoot tin cans. Playing basketball or taking tae kwon do lessons don't quite do it."

She nodded thoughtfully.

"Now don't take that to mean I don't think the troops have the worst end of the whole deal, because they sure as hell do. We had it easy by comparison. I'm just saying that we medics see all the carnage, and even if we want to go shoot something up, we'll never get a chance. I guess we're not supposed to get angry, or if we do, we're supposed to channel it into saving lives."

"We probably do channel most of it that way. But there are still times…" And she could remember more than one.

"Exactly. But let's not ruin this fantastic evening by continuing down this particular trail. Can you shake free?"

She lifted her head from his shoulder and looked at him. In that instant, she knew she could shake free just by looking at him. He took her to a whole other level.

"I can," she said and smiled. "When I look at you."

"Same here," he said, his tone dropping, his voice growing husky. "When I look at you, I see all the promise that was sucked out of my life long ago."

He leaned slowly toward her, as if he were going to kiss her.

At that moment, however, there was a hard hammering on her door.

"Sheriff," said a too-familiar voice. "Open up."

Krissie jumped up. "Oh, God, I'm not dressed."

"You run into your room and find your clothes. I'll get the door."

She grabbed her clothes from the floor and dashed into her bedroom, closing the door just as the hammering started again.

She hoped to God something terrible hadn't happened.

"We're here to take you in for questioning in the deaths of two hospital patients," Deputy Sara Ironheart said. Just past her shoulder stood Deputy Jake Lancaster. Krissie knew both of them, but it didn't make her feel any better.

For the first time in her life, she discovered what it felt like. Two deputies standing before her to take her to the sheriff's office, all the doorways along the hall open as her neighbors watched. Knowing her own innocence didn't ease the sense of shame and humiliation.

"Can I ride along?" David asked from behind her.

"No, doctor," Sara said evenly. "You can follow in your own vehicle if you wish."

Then Sara's gaze trained on Krissie again. "Are you coming?"

Apparently Gage had put his plan into action with a vengeance, Krissie thought miserably. She couldn't imagine ever holding her head up again in this town after this. "Do you need to handcuff me?"

"No, ma'am, this is just for questioning."

Turning, Krissie slipped on the shoes she kept by the door, gave a longing and sad look to David, then turned to go with the deputies.

She felt like she was on a perp walk, as her neighbors watched her go by. The only bright spot was David calling after her, "I'll be there in five minutes, Krissie!"

Downstairs, outside, the flashing lights of the squad car had drawn even more of the curious. Probably an additional fillip to Gage's plan. The more attention he drew, the faster the rumor would get out.

At that moment, a nice, dark, dank cave would have been a welcome alternative.

Sara put her in the backseat, behind the cage, then with one whoop of the siren to warn people to stand back, they began to the drive to the sheriff's office.

"That was *not* fun," Krissie remarked grimly.

"It never is," Sara answered. But her voice had gentled from a tone of severe authority. "It'll be okay."

"After that," Krissie retorted, "it'll never be okay again."

She was absolutely convinced of that. She couldn't imagine any way this could play out now, even with nailing the real criminal, that wouldn't leave her tainted in the eyes of the county.

Where there's smoke there's fire. How many times had she heard that in her life? Nothing Gage said now would ever completely erase the impression people would have that Kristin Tate was somehow involved in those murders. Why the hell had she agreed to this?

But before despair could overtake her, she felt her spine stiffen. She'd faced a lot worse to save lives, a lot worse than a few rumors and sidelong looks. Lives hung in the balance here, and it was important to catch this predator before someone else died.

She could handle this. She didn't have to like it, but she could handle it.

She recited that mantra all the way to the sheriff's office. She could handle this.

They put her in an interrogation room near the back of the building. No windows, but totally out of place, there was a cot against one wall that looked as if it had been freshly made. A coffeepot sat on a small table in the corner with a stack of cups, sugar, creamer and artificial sweetener. There was even a tray of sandwiches and another of Danishes under plastic wrap on the long table that had a chair on either side.

The door opened and Gage stepped in. "I know it's

not the Hilton," he said, waving his arm to indicate the amenities, "but it's as comfortable as I can make things here. The cameras and microphones are turned off, so you have privacy. You know where the bathroom is, and you won't be locked in, okay?"

She nodded, still standing in the center of the room. "Do you have *any* idea how awful that was?"

He nodded. "Can you think of a faster way to get the rumor out?"

"My mother is going to have a cow."

"Actually," said the familiar voice of her dad, "she's not." He stepped around the corner and joined her and Gage in the small room.

"*Et tu, Brute?*" she asked sarcastically.

He gave her an almost mischievous smile, one she hadn't seen in many years. "Yeah, me too. You do what's necessary, and I think this is necessary. So does your mom. Honey, we've got to catch this guy before he does anything else. Before *you* get hurt."

"I think I've just been mortally wounded. I'll never be able to hold my head up again."

"Sure you will," her dad said bracingly. "Don't catastrophize."

How many times had he said that to her, especially during her teen years?

"Being carted off by the cops in front of several dozen neighbors isn't exactly catastrophizing."

Gage spoke. "No handcuffs, remember? You'll have to trust me on this, Krissie. There won't be a word spoken against you once we get the guy."

"How are you going to achieve that?"

"For now, that has to be my little secret."

"Great."

Nate cleared his throat. "There's a young doctor out front demanding to see you. I get the feeling his interest is no longer purely professional."

Krissie glared at him. "So?"

Nate shrugged. "I think I should leave now so that when your mother asks me for all the details I don't have to lie about the fact that you're not in this room alone all night." He closed the distance between them, hugged her tight and whispered in her ear, "Trust us, sugar. Trust us. It will all come out right."

She wouldn't have believed those words from any other soul on the planet, but from her dad, well, that was different. "I love you, Daddy," she murmured, as her throat tightened and stupid tears pricked her eyes.

"I know you do, sugar. So just hang in there." He gave her another squeeze and walked out. She could hear his steps fade away down the hall.

That left her and Gage, and he was half smiling. "I'll let David back here in just a minute. The only restriction you have is not to go in the front office where you could be seen from the street. Sara and I are going to hang out here, like we're questioning you, but basically we're going to be napping in the back office. Around eight tomorrow morning, when there are enough people heading for work and thus plenty of people to see you, you'll be free to go."

"I have to stay all night?"

"Well, we made a big to-do about taking you in. I want just as much notice when we take you home. That should frustrate our killer and push him."

"If that's what's pushing him."

"If it's not, we'll know pretty quick."

"And then?"

He shook his head. "One step at a time, Krissie. If there's one thing I've learned in this business, you can't plan too far down the road, because you keep finding out new things, and plans go out the window like birds in flight."

She nodded then, resigning herself.

"Oh, and while I didn't say anything to your dad, there *is* another cot free. You want David in here with you tonight?"

She looked at him and saw only the greatest kindness there. A far cry from a man who had once scared her because death seemed to look out of those eyes. "Actually," she said, "if David wants to be here, then yes. And I don't care who knows." The last was a small jab at her dad, and Gage chuckled.

"Whatever," he said. "It's not like Emma and I observed the rules of bundling before we got married. We'll get that cot in here."

A minute later, David joined her. Once again, he looked like the disheveled and overworked doctor she had seen on her first shift: hair tousled, beard unshaven and growing dark, and his eyes almost hollow.

"God," he said, stepping into the room and wrapping her instantly in a bear hug. "God! Even knowing it wasn't for real, it was hell."

"I know. I felt so humiliated."

"How could you not, with all those people staring as if you were a sideshow. At least they didn't cuff you."

"Small favors," she murmured. Pressing her face into his shoulder, she inhaled deeply of his scent. He was better than aromatherapy. Relaxation seeped through her.

From the doorway came the sound of a clearing

throat. Krissie at once started to step back, but David held on.

"Just a folding cot," Gage said. "Sorry it's not better, but it's all we've got."

"It'll do," David said. "I can sleep on the floor if necessary."

Krissie turned her head to smile at Gage, resting her cheek against David's shoulder. "Thanks, Gage."

"Not a problem. But after this, I'll owe you one."

"Yeah," she said, still smiling, "you might at that."

Gage quickly unfolded the wooden cot, locked it in place. "I'll be back in a second with some blankets and pillows from the jail upstairs. Just ignore me."

David grinned. "I was planning to do exactly that."

But after a quick kiss, he released Krissie and pulled out a chair at the table. "Maybe I should ask if he has some spare handcuffs." He wiggled his brows. "We could take turns."

Krissie finally laughed, letting go of the last of the unhappy feelings from her public humiliation. She pulled out the other chair and sat facing David. "You aren't a sheriff's daughter, so you wouldn't know those are exactly the wrong kind of cuffs."

"Are they? What's wrong with them?"

"Metal. They can hurt you in short order."

"I hadn't thought of that." He lifted one eyebrow. "And how did you learn this?"

"I played with them when I was a kid. Snuck them off my dad's belt. Then, because I'd been bad, I didn't want to go to him for help when I realized they were too tight and the more I struggled the more I abraded my wrists."

"Ouch." He winced. "I can just see it."

She lifted one corner of her mouth in a smile. "So, if you want to play with cuffs, I recommend leather, maybe with fur lining."

He leaned toward her, his voice going husky. "Oh, lady, we may have to make a trip to the big bad city and do a little naughty shopping."

She giggled. "I might be persuaded."

"Somehow I think that won't be too hard." He reached out and she placed her hand in his. "The worst part of tonight is going to be that we're both night owls. How much easier if we could just sleep through our incarceration."

"Somebody gave me a couple of really good sleeping pills earlier," she said coyly. "Funny, they wore off when the cops arrived."

"Only a couple. I could have sworn the dose was higher."

At that she broke into a laugh. From down the hallway she heard footsteps. "Shh," she said, still laughing.

Gage appeared with pillows and blankets tucked under his arms. "Now don't have too much fun," he said as he dropped his load on the cot. "You're being interrogated, remember. The third degree. Bright lights. Nasty cops shouting at you."

Krissie's look questioned him. "Have you ever done that?"

"In my younger, seedier days." Apparently sensing the invitation, he perched on the edge of the table. "You are full of questions."

"Well—" she hesitated "—I've always been a little curious since you were an undercover agent with the DEA."

He shrugged his shoulder, then winced. Along with

his burn scars, he still limped and had a notoriously bad back. "Well, it's not exactly like the movies."

"I didn't think it would be."

"In a way, the worst part wasn't the undercover work itself. Yeah, it sometimes leaves you feeling really soiled, but that's inescapable. For me, at the beginning at least, it was that other agents and cops didn't know who I was. So they were after me, too, and sometimes *they* didn't follow the letter of the law."

"How so?"

He cocked his head. "I got roughed up a few times. Manhandled. Clubbed on a traffic stop."

"My God!" Krissie said. "I hope you reported these guys."

"I couldn't. Besides, it helped establish my bona fides with the guys I was after. It got kind of annoying though, when they'd put me under surveillance and threaten to blow my whole gig. *That* was when I had to call my handler, and he'd had to find some way to call the dogs off without giving my identity away."

"That must have been hard."

"Harder for him than me. Overall though, that kind of stuff didn't happen often. I had more trouble with local cops than DEA."

"Why is that?"

"Because DEA was after bigger fish. The locals were after anything they could find, from users to street dealers. When I got far enough up in the local organization and started wearing fancy suits, I think everybody was watching me." He chuckled. "The game got real interesting at times."

"How long did you do that?"

"About five years. Then we had the goods, and I had

to blow my cover by testifying in court." His face darkened then, but he apparently forced himself to move away from that as he rose. "Anyway, you can stay under cover only so long in most cases. There comes a point where you can be pinpointed by what you've revealed to the authorities, or when you just have to come out and testify to make the case. Yeah, they try to protect you, even in court, but the secret is pretty much out, so you move on to other work in the agency at a different location, and some new young agent comes along to replace you."

He managed a crooked smile as he started toward the door. "It's not a life I would recommend to anyone, but I sure as hell thought I was hot stuff when I was doing it."

Then he was gone, closing the door behind him.

"Wow," David said quietly. "I never thought of being victimized by other cops."

"Me, either, but I guess it makes sense. How many people can you afford to have knowing who the under-cover guys are?"

"Not many, would be my guess. With each additional person who knows, there's that much more chance some-one will slip."

"Yeah." She thought about that. "I wonder if there are different degrees of being under cover?"

"Probably. But Gage would be the one to ask about that. But DEA…" He shook his head. "I hear they're more likely to get killed on the job than any other area of law enforcement."

"It wouldn't surprise me." What did surprise her was that she suddenly yawned.

David's eyes creased with a smile. "Maybe you *can* sleep through your interrogation."

"It's beginning to feel possible. Except that now I'm hungry." She eyed the trays. "I *should* have a sandwich."

"You're more likely to sleep if you eat a Danish. Carbs make you sleepy."

She started to shake her head, but she couldn't deny that a raspberry Danish was looking very attractive right now.

"Go on," David said. "I'll join you. Moderation will never kill you. You know that."

So they peeled back the plastic from the pastry tray. They used napkins from the coffee bar as plates, and moments later, Krissie was savoring the incredible flavor and richness.

"This," she said, "has to be five mortal sins at least."

David grinned. "This kind of sin is meant to be enjoyed."

"I wonder if Sara or Gage would like some?"

"You want me to ask? Maybe throw a short party?"

"I feel as if I should ask."

At that, his grinned broadened. "Tell me why you should feel like acting hostess when you're being held unwillingly in an interrogation room?"

She had to smile too. "I guess you can blame my mother. For her, food means socializing. You can't go into her house without being fed."

"But this is different."

"I know. But somehow the imperative is working in reverse."

He outright laughed. "Okay, I'll see if anyone wants anything."

Which was how the four of them came to have a party. They made coffee, enjoyed the food platters, and wiled away the wee hours telling old, bad jokes and listening to Sara reminisce about the county's good old days.

Or at least she indulged them with the notion, because as she finally said, "The good old days really weren't all that different. Oh, we had fewer people. You remember, Krissie. Time was, our total population was around five thousand. Now it's creeping close to eight. Still small enough to know most everyone, though."

"If you're a cop," David replied.

"Or a doctor," Gage retorted.

"Regardless," Krissie interjected, "my dad's been saying this place is going to hell in a handbasket ever since I can remember."

"Probably," Sara answered, "because he remembers an even earlier time than we do. Back when this town basically had one main street, a drive-in theater and enough bars to give the cowpokes plenty of fuel to get in trouble on payday."

"They were still doing that when I was little," Krissie told David. "Just not in town."

"Nope," Sara agreed. "Your dad had a lot to do with moving most of the bars out of the city. We still have Mahoney's of course, but most of the dancing and drinking business happens at the roadhouses." She smiled faintly. "That's where I met Gideon, you know."

Krissie's eyebrows lifted. "Really? At a roadhouse?"

"Well, some of the patrons objected to his heritage. Seems they didn't want to drink with a Native American. When I got there, he was standing in the middle of a crowd of men who were hell bent on beating him half to death." She shook her head. "First time I fired my shotgun on duty."

"I'll bet that got their attention."

"That it did." Sara smiled. "I sure did like the look of that guy. He was ready to take on the world."

Krissie propped her chin in her hand. "So what did you do?"

"I got his butt the hell out of there. What else was I going to do? One of me wasn't enough to arrest all of them, and there was no way I was going to leave him there, even if he wanted the brawl almost as much as they did. Gideon's always been a fighter. And I don't mean in the sense of beating people up. He'll work harder than ten men to prove himself, and he won't take any crap. Those idiots picked the wrong man to mess with."

Then Sara laughed and reached for another sand-wich. "I would never have guessed from that first meeting that he can gentle the wildest horse with a murmur and a touch."

"Sometimes," Gage remarked, "people can surprise you in the best ways."

Krissie looked at David, thinking that yes, maybe people could. Because David was not at all what she had expected from their first meeting.

Who would have thought it?

Chapter 12

Gage insisted on taking her back to her apartment in a patrol car, so as to gain maximum attention. He picked the right time, too, though, given his job, Krissie supposed she shouldn't be surprised.

Just before eight o'clock, the car pulled up at the apartment house. It seemed like even more people were in the parking lot than last night, getting ready to leave for work, and Jake Lancaster's judicious use of flashers brought even more to the windows. She had even seen people in their cars craning their necks to look at her as they passed.

Juicy gossip indeed: the former sheriff's daughter taken in for questioning and held all night. Most people wouldn't know about the murders, but that didn't matter. According to Gage, there was only one person who needed to put things together.

"Be careful tonight," he had warned her before she

left. "Get plenty of rest. I'm going to need you to be on high alert."

She gave him a humorless smile. "That's what I usually am on the job."

He touched her arm, expression deeply serious. "I need even more than that tonight, Krissie. Watch everything, everyone. I'm going to have people there."

"They'll stand out like sore thumbs. Everyone knows everyone, Gage!"

"Trust me. I'll tell you about it later. Now get some rest. I need to talk with David for a few before he follows you home."

She went. Jake went inside with her, drawing even more attention, and refused to leave until David returned. His strong face framed an apologetic smile. "Orders," he said.

Fatigued beyond belief, she simply nodded and went to her bedroom, where she collapsed on the air mattress and fell into a dreamless, exhausted sleep.

When she awoke mid afternoon, David was lying on the floor beside her air mattress, sound asleep. The instant she tried to rise, however, the mattress made that awful, hollow sound, like fingers being dragged roughly over a balloon, and his eyes popped open.

"Let me make coffee," he said. "We've got to talk."

Her answer was hesitant and a bit drowsy. "Okay."

"Go take a shower. Gage filled me in."

But she still hesitated. "You look awful. Didn't you sleep?"

"I had some stuff to do. Now go shower while I make coffee." He yawned and offered a smile. "We've been busy. Don't you want to know?"

That was enough to galvanize her. She hopped into the shower, scrubbing, rinsing, washing her hair in record time. She even resented the time it took to towel off and dress. Finally, she was going to know the plan.

With a towel wrapped around her head, she emerged from the bedroom just as David was putting two mugs of coffee on the table. Apparently they'd sent the extra sandwiches and Danish home with him, because there they sat on one of her plates.

The first thing he did was open his arms. She walked into them, drew a deep breath of contentment, and lifted her mouth for his kiss. He spared nothing, kissing her like a starved man. But finally he drew back, sighing heavily. "Not now, honey. We've got to talk first."

She sat at the table, feeling curiosity rise again, apparently only partially damped by his touch and kiss. "So what's going on?"

He took the chair facing her. "The hospital is going to be loaded with cops tonight."

"But I already told Gage they'll stick out like sore thumbs! Everyone will notice them."

He shook his head. "Gage isn't dumb. These won't be local people. He's asked for some help from other agencies. They're going to be sifting into the hospital all day. What's more, you're going to find a big change on your floor."

"How so?"

"None of your patients will be alone in their rooms by the time your shift begins."

"Are you moving people?"

He shook his head. "I spent the morning and early afternoon admitting a whole bunch of people at Gage's request. There's a whole gamut of ailments, as you'll see. But most are going to be in the rooms with your other patients, and they're all cops."

Krissie brightened. "That'll keep my patients safe." But then a thought made her frown. "But what if the guy is afraid to move when there are two patients in a room."

"Thought of that, too. One or two of the cops will be solo in their rooms. A man and a woman, I think Gage said. Two easy potential victims, and they can't be roomed together."

Krissie nodded. "Good thinking. But how are we treating them?"

David smiled. "I'm brilliant."

"Yeah?"

"Yeah. They all have the requisite saline IVs, but other than that, every one of them has been prescribed oral medication, which they know not to swallow."

She started to smile too. "Absolutely no reason to pump anything in the IVs."

"Exactly. As for the *real* patients, I sent two to another wing because they need ongoing treatment. But for the rest, I've ordered treatments withdrawn for tonight. Not one of them is getting anything by IV or injection."

"Is it safe?"

"Most of them are ready to go home. Word on the floor is they're just being observed prior to release."

"It'll work," she said with sudden certainty.

David nodded but said, "It better, because I don't know if I can arrange this for another night. God, I had no idea how difficult it could be to play chess with hospital patients."

She gave a small silent laugh. "Well, I don't think that's how we're expected to operate."

He reached out and touched her cheek gently with his fingertips. "God willing, we'll finish this tonight. Then everything can go back to normal."

Normal? Yes, it would be nice not to have this threat hanging over her head and the heads of her patients, but what did David mean by normal? He could go back to his place and she to hers, and follow their separate lives. Her stomach sank at the mere thought. All the things they had talked about doing together, what if those went away too? What if last night had simply been passion born of adrenaline and nothing else?

Then, even as she was sinking, she had a sudden thought. "You were supposed to see that contractor today!"

"No worries. I *am* good." He winked. "I called and postponed for a couple of days. We'll probably talk to him on Friday."

We'll probably talk to him. At least that held out some ray of hope.

But then she shook herself with annoyance. For a person who had once owned a sunny temperament, she had certainly become a Gloomy Gus.

"If you don't want to eat leftovers," he said, "I can make a meal."

"I honestly don't know that I could eat. My stomach is currently full of butterflies." And lead weights, but she didn't want to mention those.

"Maybe later," he said. "But I'm not letting you go to work without some food in you. You're going to need all your energy."

"Look, I can take care of my own diet!" The flare-up seemed to come out of nowhere, even to her. He looked taken aback, but before she could find a way to apologize, he was already making excuses.

"Sorry," he said. "It's the doctor thing. I just get so used to giving people directions."

"No," she said swiftly. "No. My fault. I was reacting from nerves. Reacting to something else."

He waited for her to continue, but when she didn't he prodded. "Something else? Or someone else?"

She bit her lip. God, she hated to even think about it, let alone discuss it, because she always felt so bad about herself when she did. Yet she realized that even though she thought she'd broken some barriers yesterday, there was still a lot of detritus that would keep popping up from the depths for a while. And if she hoped not to drive David away, he deserved an explanation for these moments.

"I was reacting to Al," she said finally.

"The mysterious ex?"

"The same." She looked away, not wanting to see his reaction. "Alvin Tyler. Ex, but not soon enough. I get embarrassed by how long I put up with him. He never hit me or anything, he wasn't the type. But he had other ways. And he was a control freak." She touched her hair. "See these blond streaks? *Not* my idea, and they can't grow out fast enough. I still can't believe I put up with it."

"Maybe," David said gently, "you were too wounded to put up a fight."

She shrugged one shoulder. "Maybe. Blame it on whatever. But the fact is that I stayed far too long, and let him rule far too much, from what I wore to what I ate, to who I could be friends with. Dammit, David, I couldn't even pick a TV show."

"I'm sorry. That must have been horrible."

"He made me feel as if I *couldn't* do those things capably. And then…oh, this is so hard to admit."

"What?"

"When I finally got enough sense together to realize what he'd done to me, and I moved out, I found myself totally paralyzed."

"In what ways?"

She looked at him then, giving him an almost bitter smile. "Bet you never guessed that it could be impossible to choose from a restaurant menu. Or decide to buy a piece of furniture. Or select a CD to listen to."

All of a sudden, she saw the light go on in his face as understanding dawned.

"Oh, God, Krissie," he said quietly. "Oh, God, that's awful."

"Yeah, it was. And still sometimes is. I'm still uncomfortable in a restaurant. I don't own a TV. I sleep on the floor. I'm okay on the job, but that's the *only* place he didn't manage to damage my confidence."

He reached out, almost cautiously, to take her hand. "Seems to me you're making big strides." He pointed to the table, the couch, the chair.

"Baby steps," she said.

"Big baby steps."

She released a long breath. "So okay, now you know the whole ugly story. I'm not sure how I got into it, but I know how I got out of it."

"How?"

"I woke up one morning and something told me to run. The first place I ran was to a friend at work. She got me an immediate appointment with the staff psychiatrist, who listened to me, questioned me, and after about two sessions, told me to move out immediately. Then he called my friend in and told her to make sure I did, and that I didn't tell Al where I was going."

"Good shrink, great friend."

Krissie nodded. "The best. Both of them. She found the apartment for me, rented it in her name, gave me a few things to get by with, and even dragged me out to get a new cell phone. I never heard from Al again, except once when he accosted me outside work."

"What happened then?"

She managed a smile. "I discovered I had more than one friend. A couple of them were rather big vets who threatened to beat him to death with their crutches if he came near me again. The other one, who was in a wheelchair, vowed he'd leave tire tracks on Al after the other two knocked him down."

David suddenly grinned and started clapping his hands. "I'd love to meet all these folks."

"I still keep in touch with all of them. I was thinking about inviting them up here after I get more settled."

"I think that would be a great idea." His eyes were warm, and she didn't see any disapproval or disgust there. None of the emotions she still sometimes felt for herself.

"Anyway, another six months in Denver, another six months of therapy, and here I am."

At that his smile faded a bit. "You're sure it's not Al?"

She nodded. "He just didn't think that way. I never saw a hint, not the slightest hint, that he was capable of physical violence."

"So you said before." His gaze grew distant and thoughtful, but only for a few moments. Then he came back to her. "Guess we'll find out soon, and get this monkey off your back."

"I hope so," she said. "God, I hope so."

David needed a nap, so they curled up on her air mattress. It was a tight fit, but neither of them minded it at all. In fact, Krissie enjoyed having her back to him and his arms around her. Eventually, however, when he at last loosened his hold and fell into a deep sleep, she slipped away because she was simply too antsy to hold still.

The night shift loomed in front of her with all kinds of nerve-wracking possibilities. Much as she wanted to believe that Gage had covered every base, she knew only too well that things could go wrong, things that hadn't been planned for or even considered possible.

SNAFU didn't apply only to the military.

But even as she busied herself making lunches for them both to take to work, and something for a light supper, she couldn't stop dreading the hours ahead. They loomed like a dark tunnel that no light could truly penetrate.

She hated that feeling, and no amount of familiarity would ever make her comfortable with those times when she feared something bad was going to happen but she couldn't guess where it would come from.

Tonight was certainly one of those nights. Although, she thought as she started making a tuna and macaroni salad, maybe the worst thing that could happen was nothing at all. The killer had taken no action during her last two shifts. Maybe he'd done whatever he wanted and was gone. Maybe she was only a coincidental victim in his insane plot, not an intended target.

Perish the thought! They needed to get this guy, and if she was only a peripheral accident to whatever he intended, she couldn't imagine where they could look next.

The breeze kicked up, warm and dry, and tossed the curtains at her living room windows, reminding her how much she loved summers here. Sometimes they got too hot, but mostly brought the kind of weather that made you want to get out and do things.

That breeze carried her back to her childhood, when this kind of weather virtually guaranteed a backyard picnic, or an afternoon of badminton on the grass. Long, lazy bike rides with her friends gathering together under a tree to talk about all the things teens find so important.

A time when she had felt not only loved, but utterly safe.

Maybe those times would come again.

Then strong arms closed around her from behind, and with a sigh, she sank back against David.

"Hi," he murmured, his breath warm against her neck.

She turned, lifting her arms, welcoming him in a warm embrace. "Hi," she murmured back, and kissed him with every hope in her heart.

When their mouths separated, he looked deep into her eyes. "It's going to be okay," he promised.

But the assurance didn't seem to matter any more, as he scooped her up in her arms and carried her to the air mattress.

Other things, matters of life, were for now more important than the night ahead.

Chapter 13

They drove to the hospital separately, a conscious decision made because no one could know what the night might hold. A quick kiss, touch and look in the parking lot, then they headed their separate ways.

Krissie changed into fresh scrubs in the women's locker room, pausing reluctantly to run a brush quickly through her hair. Now that it was time, she felt eager to get this night started.

As she walked to her wing, she waved and smiled at people she passed, ignoring the odd looks some of them gave her. Gage's rumor had grown the legs he expected. She could practically read it verbatim from some of the expressions.

Keeping a smile on her face, she made her way to the nurses' station. Julie and Nancy had their heads together in conversation as she approached, but fell abruptly silent when they saw her.

Still smiling, she joined them. "I hear we have some additional patients tonight."

The two women exchanged looks, then Julie nodded and spoke. "A *lot*," she said. "But nobody is very sick."

"That's good. Can I see the records?"

Nancy hopped back from the computer screen. Just as Krissie was settling into the chair to read, the nurse she was relieving came up.

"Hey, Krissie," said Wanda Pennington. "How's it going?"

"Been better," Krissie said truthfully, figuring she had to at least act as if she'd spent all night being questioned about two murders.

Wanda leaned over the counter and smiled. "Don't let it get to you. Not your fault you were on shift when those two patients died."

"That's kind of my feeling," Krissie said. "Except I feel bad we couldn't save them."

"Happens," Wanda said. "You've been a nurse long enough to know." Then she looked at Julie and Nancy. "These two, of course, are full of salacious details about something about which they know *nothing*."

Krissie wondered why Wanda was being so blunt. "I guess a lot of people are curious."

"Probably," Wanda sniffed. "But most should know better. Have a good night. I just hope all these patients don't start feeling ignored and ringing their bells. If they do, make Julie and Nancy do the running. They deserve it."

With a toss of her head, Wanda headed off.

Krissie turned to look at her two LPNs. "Want to talk to me about it?"

They both hesitated as if they'd been caught with their hands in the cookie jar. Finally Nancy screwed up the courage. "We were just wondering why the sheriff should take you in like that."

"Can't talk about it," Krissie said. "But as you see, I'm *here*."

Point made and taken, the two women looked deflated. "Yeah," said Julie. "Sorry. We were just curious."

"Everybody gets curious," Krissie said smoothly. She turned back to the monitor to read the charts. Everything appeared to be just fine, including the influx of patients all admitted that day by David. Satisfied the evening should progress without problems of the natural kind, she rose and announced she was going to make her rounds.

Down at the far end of the hall she saw the orderly— Charlie, that was it—mopping steadily away.

She moved from room to room, checking on the real patients, pretending to check on the new patients. A little conversation, a touch-up here and there on the beds, letting everyone know who she was, making sure the last meal trays had been removed.

That's when she realized this was going to be a long night. The murderer struck in the small hours of the morning, not during the evening, and all she had was a ward full of people who weren't sick, or who should be going home in the morning.

"Lovely," she muttered under her breath. If the hands of the clock could move any slower, she didn't know how.

She punctiliously updated every chart, spending

more time than necessary at the job while Julie and Nancy circulated, keeping an eye on visitors who should be leaving soon.

The ward emptied finally, and it was time for the ten o'clock meds. Easy enough. Nobody seemed to need anything except a sleeping pill, and in one case, a mild laxative pill. As the registered nurse, she was the one who handed out the medicines, so that allowed her to let the cops in each room ditch the prescribed pills. She dropped the medicine cups in the wastebasket by the bed, but dropped the pills into the biohazard bins on the wall near their beds. Each of them, male and female alike, gave her a nod that she supposed was meant to be reassuring.

The *real* patients on the other hand were wanting a bit more attention. Why not? Nobody lying in a hospital bed wanted to feel ignored, even when they were going home in the morning.

So she sat and chatted with them, found them fresh magazines where possible, helped them find something better on TV, brought them juice and ice water.

God, some nights were boring, even when the anticipation of something horrible made your skin want to crawl.

When she finally returned to the nurses' station, she found Julie, Nancy and Charlie engaged in a game of hearts. They offered to deal her in, but she pointed out that she had to make sure she recorded all the meds.

So they scooted out of the way and let her check to make sure she hadn't skipped any entries in the room terminals. Of course she hadn't. She knew she hadn't. She just couldn't imagine trying to focus on a game of cards right now.

This waiting was killing her.

At midnight, Charlie said good night and departed.

At two, nothing had happened.

At three, she began to feel wound up as tight as a spring. She told Julie and Nancy to take their breaks. Only one of them went, of course. They knew she wasn't supposed to be left alone. Hadn't Dr. Marcus made that the rule only a few days ago?

Krissie wanted to pull her own hair.

But finally, there came an urge she couldn't postpone. "Julie, I have to run to the rest room."

"Go ahead. I can keep an eye on everything." Julie smiled. "It's a quiet night, right?"

Too quiet, in a way. Krissie darted into the staff bathroom that was right behind the nurses' station. Safe enough, because Julie had seen where she had gone. David's edict was being followed.

She hurried through her business, scrubbing her hands with added effort to speed the process. It couldn't have been more than two minutes.

When she emerged, Julie was gone from the station. A call light was blinking from a couple of rooms down the hall, bed B. Julie had probably gone to answer it.

But wait. Her heart froze. Wasn't bed B the cop?

Krissie followed immediately, in case something was wrong. She peeked into the room to find no one but the two patients there. A quick check revealed that the real one was sleeping, and the cop was awake. His eyes followed her as she checked the other patient.

She paused by the bed. "Did you hit the call button? It's on for your bed."

The cop shook his head. "Maybe I rolled on it. I'm getting stiff from lying here and I was tossing a bit."

"Can I get you anything?"

"I'm fine, really."

Reaching over his head, she turned off the call. "Well," she murmured with a smile, "you know how to get me if you need me."

He grinned back at her.

So where was Julie? Probably answering a call and had already turned off the call light.

She went down the hall, checking the rooms on the right first. As she entered the last room, the one with the female police officer in it, she pushed the door open a hair and saw someone standing near the bed.

The light coming from night lights near the base of the wall didn't exactly illuminate things above foot level.

"Julie?" she said, although almost instantly she realized it wasn't Julie at all.

She stepped into the room just as the person beside the bed turned toward her.

"Charlie? What are you doing here…?"

The words barely escaped her mouth before Charlie grabbed her, whirled her around with an arm behind her back. In horror, she felt the prick of a needle at her neck, not puncturing, just threatening.

And there, on the floor under the cop's bed, was another of those dolls. "Charlie, what…?"

"Shut up."

Apparently the woman on the bed had dozed off, which she wasn't supposed to do. She stirred now, mumbling, and tried to sit up.

She's drugged, Krissie realized in horror. But she was sure she had tossed the sleeping pill into the biohazard container.

"Charlie…"

"I said 'shut up.' She won't be able to help you, so shut up."

"What did you do to her?"

"It's so easy to put something in their water."

Oh, God! Krissie felt a sudden chill run through her. They were thinking of everything else, assuming the murderer would just slip in and inject through the IV port. It hadn't occurred to anyone that he might give his victim an added sedative in the water.

"Oh, dear God," Krissie whispered. "That's why Mrs. Alexander was so sleepy!"

"You think I want them to suffer? The way my brother suffered?"

"What are you talking about?"

At that instant, with a Herculean effort, the female cop reached the call button and hit it. From down the hall, Krissie could hear the buzz.

"Dammit," Charlie said. He twisted her arm even harder and turned her around, pushing her toward the door, the needle still at her neck. If that syringe contained the potassium she suspected, the injection would be as good as a bullet to the brain.

As he shoved her into the hallway, Julie emerged from the room across the way and let out a scream.

"Shut up or I'll stab her," Charlie growled.

Julie immediately clapped her hand to her mouth, silencing the scream. She stood frozen.

Charlie started pushing Krissie toward the door at the end of the hall, away from the nurses' station. As a nurse attached to the Marine Corps, she'd received some good military training. Self-defense training. And nursing had made her strong.

As they turned, with the first sounds of pounding

footsteps coming up the hall behind them, she simultaneously jammed her heel hard on the arch of his foot and reached up with her free hand, sliding it between her and his arm, the one that held the needle to her throat. She grabbed his thumb and yanked it backward. She felt the needle scrape her neck but not puncture.

In that instant of unexpected, extraordinary pain, his grip on her other arm loosened and the needle clattered to the floor. She yanked loose and whirled away in time to see the cavalry racing down the hall in answer to Julie's scream.

David was there, too, as if he had been waiting for this along with the cops, and there was murder in his eyes.

Charlie started to dive for the syringe, but Krissie kicked it away and then the pack of cops and David landed on him.

"We've got him," one of the cops said.

Shaking but inwardly steady, at least for the moment, Krissie turned to David, who was rising to his feet and still looking ready to kill. "We've got to help the female cop. He dosed her with a sedative and I don't know how much."

David visibly got a grip on himself and took charge instantly, telling Julie what to get. Krissie started to follow him into the room but he ordered her out.

Before she could argue, Micah appeared beside her, taking her arm. "Other medicos are coming," he said. "You need to sit this one out."

Just how badly, she didn't realize until she started to sit at the nurses' station and her legs turned to rubber. She dropped onto the chair like lead.

"You're as white as a sheet," Micah said. He squatted

beside her. "Lower your head, Krissie. David's got everything in hand. You know you can trust him."

For once, she did as she was told without resenting it. Leaning forward, she brought her head to below heart level.

"It's fun when the adrenaline drops off abruptly," he said. "You'll be better in a minute. Damn, girl, I'm proud of how you handled that."

She turned her head toward him, hugging her knees like a lifeline. "But why?" she asked. "Why?"

Micah's expression grew grim. "That's exactly what we're going to find out."

Several hours later, long after an on-call nurse had relieved her of duty, long after the scratch on her neck was treated, long after David had dragged her to the break room to eat the tuna sandwich and raw carrots she'd packed for lunch and never tasted, only after he watched her eat every single bite and had assured himself that she was neither in shock nor likely to go into shock now, was she allowed to leave the hospital and go to the sheriff's office.

David drove her, reminding her they could come back for her car later. Just as she was beginning to resent feeling as if everyone were trying to wrap her in cotton wool, they walked into the sheriff's office to find the place crawling with cops, many of whom had recently been playing patient. They were sucking down coffee and helping each other write reports.

Gage spied her and motioned her back to his office. The only other person there, besides her and David, was Micah. Micah sat on the edge of table in the corner, having nudged some papers aside with his hip, and was sipping coffee. He smiled with his eyes when he saw her.

Gage motioned her and David to chairs facing his desk, then he went around to take his own seat, judiciously arranging the pillows as he did so.

"Okay," he said.

"Okay?" Krissie repeated. "I don't see anything okay about this. Did you find out why he did it?"

"Clams talk more than this guy." He shook his head. "I'm letting him cool his heels a bit, then I'm going to ask you for a big favor."

She eyed him questioningly.

"After you help me make out a report about exactly what happened on your end, I want you to talk to him."

"Me?"

"If he's going to talk at all," Gage said, "it'll probably be to the person he was really after, which seems to be you."

She nodded slowly. "He said something about his brother. And I sure as hell want to know why he did this."

"Don't we all? He's been advised of his rights, but he hasn't asked for an attorney. If I send you in there, I'm going to advise him of his rights again."

"You're sending me in alone?"

Gage nodded. "Don't worry. He's shackled to the floor, and before you get in there, he's going to be shackled to the chair as well."

She frowned. "But nothing he tells me can be used in court, can it? I mean, isn't it hearsay or something?"

"Actually, it's an exception to the hearsay rule, and you can testify in court to everything he says to you, including an admission of guilt. But we're not going to rely on that. Like I said, I'm going to advise him of his rights again, and tell him that anything he says to you can be used in court. And it's going to be on videotape as well."

She nodded. Weary as she was feeling, determination stiffened her. "This isn't going to be fun. He must really hate me. But of course I'll try to get him to talk."

"It's not essential that he tell us anything. We caught him in the act, we know he doped a cop and threatened you, the syringe contained that potassium you were telling me about, and there was a doll under Detective Sousa's bed. He's nailed. But I'd sure like to know why."

"Me, too."

One corner of Gage's mouth lifted in a slight smile. "But first I need your sworn statement about what happened tonight so no defense attorney can claim your recollections were altered by your conversation with the perp."

Her statement took the better part of an hour, in part because there weren't a whole lot of fast typists in the department.

But then, at long last, she was led back to the interrogation room. David touched her arm just before Gage opened the door to admit her.

She looked up at him.

"I'm going to be watching," he said. "If you need anything at all, if anything is too unpleasant, just say my name and I'll get you out of there."

The separation, the sense of distance from everything around her that had been protecting her since the attack, suddenly dissolved. Only in that moment did she realize that the night's events hadn't even begun to touch her.

She melted into his arms, clinging, and he held her tight, as if he never wanted to let go. "Thanks," she said shakily. "Thanks."

But finally, she had to let go. She managed a wan smile and turned to face the door. Gage searched her face, seemed satisfied, and opened it.

As he had promised, Charlie Waters was shackled to the floor and cuffed to the chair. He wouldn't get very far if he tried anything. When he saw Krissie, the look of hatred was unmistakable, and so strong that she instinctively stepped back.

"Okay," Gage said to Charlie. "I'm going to let you talk to Ms. Tate, but let me remind you of your rights, because anything you say can and will be used against you in a court of law, and this conversation will be videotaped."

Gage continued, reading the man his rights, and even going so far as to ask in so many words if he wanted an attorney first.

Waters shook his head. "A lawyer will just get in the way. I want to tell this bitch the truth."

Gage hesitated. "Maybe I should stay in here."

Krissie shook her head. "No need. I've handled worse than he can dish out."

"Okay then."

She took the chair on the far side of the table and waited until Gage had closed the door. She thought, in the deep silence, that she could almost hear the hum of the video cameras, the beat of her own heart.

Then Charlie stirred and his leg irons clanked.

"So tell me," she said, keeping her voice level. Out of sight, her hands knotted into fists.

"You killed my brother."

"I did?"

"Thomas Waters. Remember him?"

She hesitated. "Charlie, I need more information. I've taken care of thousands of people."

He leaned forward as far as he could. "At the VA hospital in Denver. Double amputee. Brain injury."

"There were a lot of those." She studied his face and suddenly knew why she had thought he was familiar. And as soon as she made that connection, she remembered his brother. "I remember. You and I talked about Conard County once or twice," she said. "Your brother wasn't doing well."

"He *died* under your care!" Charlie almost spat the words.

"Unfortunately, that happened too many times."

"Yeah. Yeah, didn't it?"

"What do you mean by that?"

Charlie's anger drew his lips back into a snarl. "Tommy died, and by the time I got to the VA and started asking questions, you were gone. Quit they said. They wouldn't answer my questions, and I couldn't find you. But I'm smart."

"I'm sure you are." She hoped he couldn't tell how hard her heart was hammering.

"I hunted up your boyfriend."

At that her heart slammed. "My boyfriend? I broke off with him ages ago."

"Yeah, but I met him once, when he came to take you to lunch. I saw you with him, I even talked to him. So I found him and I told him I wanted to know why the hell my brother died and I needed to talk to you. And you know what he said to me?"

"How could I know?"

"He said, 'Oh, you'll never find out the truth. Sometimes these doctors and nurses just off the bad cases. They call it euthanasia.'"

Krissie gasped then, and her world seemed to narrow to a pinprick of light. In what stupid moment had she trusted Al with that private fear? In what horrible moment of weakness had she even discussed with that man that upon rare occasion she thought it might have happened? Not at the VA, but in the field hospitals? God, she must have been having some kind of flashback.

Charlie suddenly sat back, looking deflated. "See, you know what I'm talking about. So my brother wasn't doing well. But he was still alive. And when your boyfriend said that, I remember you telling me not to hope too hard because Tommy had such severe seizures and they seemed to be getting worse, and then you *quit one day after he died?* Do I need a roadmap?"

Krissie fought her way back from shock, taking a deep breath and then another. Finally she said, "Oh, Charlie, I swear I never killed anyone. I swear I never did anything to hurt your brother."

For the first time a shadow of doubt crossed his face. "You did. I know you must have."

"No, I swear I never did. The last thing I did for him medically was give him an injection to stop his seizure. The very injection his doctor ordered. The very injection he had gotten during other seizures. But this time the seizure didn't stop. He quit breathing. The crash team tried to bring him back…."

Tears were running down her face now, and she didn't bother to wipe them away. "I didn't kill your brother, Charlie. War killed your brother. And I'm so, so sorry."

She saw the first tear appear on his eyelash. Just one. And in that instant, he looked so wounded and hurt that she wanted to gather him in her arms.

All of sudden, Gage was there, standing beside her, gripping her shoulder in support.

"Charlie," Gage said gently, "why did you kill those two patients?"

The young man looked up, his face slack now. "So people would see she's a murderer."

Chapter 14

The next twenty-four hours passed in a dazed blur. Krissie pulled back into some place inside herself, that place where you shut everything else out in order to deal with something too huge to grasp all at once.

Her father and mother stopped by, but only briefly, to hug her and tell her they loved her.

But David remained with her. He cancelled her shift, he was there any time she looked up, he made sure she ate. In short he babied her.

But the following morning, when she woke up and found he'd moved the Kokopelli table so it was over by the window with the curtains tossing in the morning breeze and that the thermal carafe was waiting there for her along with a mug, she started to smile again.

The delicious smell of bacon issued from the kitchen.

"And you're supposed to be a doctor," she called out.

He leaned around the corner. "Okay, I promise we'll jog it or hike it off later, but there's nothing like comfort food."

"You take too much comfort in animal fat."

"So sue me." He disappeared again for a minute, she heard a pan clatter, and then he returned with a folded newspaper. "I thought this might brighten your morning and add spice to your coffee."

He snapped it open and laid it on the table in front of her, then returned whistling to the kitchen.

The big, bold headline jumped up at her: Local nurse captures killer.

Disbelieving, she began to read. "Local nurse Kristin Tate became a hero yesterday when she assisted the sheriff's department in apprehending…"

She skipped to the next paragraph to learn that she had apparently been working undercover for the sheriff's department, risking her own life to prevent further murders.

Her jaw dropped and she looked up to find David grinning like a Cheshire cat as he leaned on the doorjamb between the living area and kitchen.

"I'm no hero," she said.

"Gage told you that you weren't going to suffer from the rumors. He kept his word. Besides, the story is all true." He started walking toward her. "You assisted, you were brave, you manhandled the bad guy pretty good for a girl—"

"For a girl?"

He started laughing. "I figured that would rile you. Truth is, Krissie, whether you want to admit it or not, you're everything the paper says. My hero." Bending, he stole a quick kiss.

"Do I smell bacon burning?"

He pulled away in an instant and ran to the kitchen.

Krissie was smiling, though, as she looked down at the paper again. The story, she thought, was embarrassingly overblown, but indeed, Gage had kept his promise. She could hold her head up, and there'd be no whispering campaign of any kind, no residue of questions to follow her through life. *Thank you, Gage.*

David returned with two plates and placed them on the table. They were both mounded with eggs, bacon and buttered toast. She started to shake her head, though a smile quivered at the corners of her mouth.

He sat facing her. "Don't even say it. My professional eye tells me that you're at least ten pounds underweight, and as you well know, being underweight can be as unhealthy as being overweight."

"And somehow that makes this a healthy breakfast?" But the smile was tugging harder at the corners of her mouth.

He grinned. "You can reform me later. Dear heart, you haven't eaten enough in the last twenty-four hours to keep a sparrow alive. So enjoy the wicked calories, and I'll promise vegetarian for dinner tonight if your conscience demands it."

"Actually, I'd like Chinese."

At that, he put his chin in his palm. "How many miles do I have to drive to get your Chinese?"

"You don't. I cook it."

"Much better for the environment. Your dad's been calling frequently. Again while you were in the shower. I told him to come on over with your mom a little later."

"Thanks. I was in such a fog yesterday, I hardly remember talking to them."

"Trust me, when it comes to your well-being, your dad and mom have very sharp eyes. I'm under orders to let you rest."

"As if you wouldn't have come up with that on your own."

"Well—" he gave a mischievous smile "—it *might* have occurred to me. But the former sheriff has been checking up to make sure I was following orders."

"He would."

"He's going to make a great father-in-law."

Krissie dropped her fork, splattering food on the table. "David…" She could only look at him, stunned.

He waved a hand. "Just let me finish. Then you can tell me to take a hike."

She barely managed a nod, as something began to crack open inside of her, something that hurt as it struggled its way out.

"I knew you were growing on me," he said, his expression serious now. "You know, sort of like mold."

She couldn't even laugh at the attempted humor. Apparently he couldn't either.

"Hell," he said, "this is a great way to start. Let me begin again." He drew a breath, then resumed.

"Okay," he said. "I knew I was getting attached to you. You may have even noticed that at one point, I tried to stay away. I figured it was all happening too fast, I didn't know you well, yada yada. You can fill in the blanks, I'm sure."

She gave him a jerky nod.

"But then…" He shrugged. "Come to the point, Marcus. The fact is, the other night when I could have lost you, I couldn't play games with myself any more. Or with you. I'm in love with you."

Krissie drew a sharp breath.

"I know I'm no catch," he went on quickly. "I've got problems. Hell, the first time I laid eyes on you, I yelled at you about something that had nothing to do with you, really, and everything to do with me. I still have flash-backs apparently. I'm crusty, and sometimes difficult, and you hardly know me. So I'm not asking you to commit to anything yet. Just give me a chance, Krissie. Give me a chance to prove myself to you. Give *us* a chance to see if your feelings for me can grow. Please."

The blossoming within her remained painful, as it fought its way past the accretion of bad experiences, past the shell she had tried to forever bury it in so she could never again be hurt.

David opened his mouth again, as if he were about to say more, but she reached across the table, took his hand, and squeezed it hard.

"I want time to get to know you," she said, holding on tight as emotions began to overwhelm her. "But…I already love you!"

And there, having said it, she released the tender bud into a full bloom of aching joy.

"I love you," she said again.

The look on his face was both dazzled and dazzling, as if he couldn't quite believe his good fortune, yet still felt a joy beyond words.

He pushed back quickly and came around the table to draw her up into his arms, hugging her so close it seemed he didn't want even a molecule of air to separate them.

"You'll have all the time you need," he said huskily, looking down into her eyes. "All the time. But I'd like a Christmas wedding."

She started to laugh, but then he stole her breath with a kiss that seemed to reach to her very soul, as if he wanted to weld them together for eternity.

When he lifted his head, she was seeing stars, the good kind.

"I kinda like that Christmas wedding idea myself," she whispered.

"See, we agree on everything important." His eyes danced, and she felt the smile grow on her face.

"When's my dad coming?"

David scooped her up into his arms and carried her to the bedroom. "I really don't care, but we have all the time we need. We have the rest of our lives."

She snuggled into his embrace, pressing her face to the side of his neck. For the first time in a long time, she was actually looking forward to the rest of her life.

How much better could it be than two hearts beating as one?

* * * * *

*Celebrate 60 years of pure reading pleasure
with Harlequin!*

To commemorate the event, Harlequin Intrigue®
is thrilled to invite you to the wedding of The
Colby Agency's J. T. Baxley and his bride, Eve
Mattson.

That is, of course, if J.T. can find the woman who
left him at the altar. Considering he's a private investigator for one of the top agencies in the
country—the best of the best—that shouldn't be
a problem. The real setback is that his bride isn't
who she appears to be…and her mysterious past
has put them both in danger.

*Enjoy an exclusive glimpse of Debra Webb's
latest addition to*
**THE COLBY AGENCY:
ELITE RECONNAISSANCE DIVISION**

THE BRIDE'S SECRETS

*Available August 2009
from Harlequin Intrigue®.*

The dark figures on the dock were still firing. The bullets cutting through the surface of the water without the warning boom of shots told Eve they were using silencers.

That was to her benefit. Silencers decreased the accuracy of every shot and lessened the range.

She grabbed for the rocks. Scrambled through the darkness. Bumped her knee on a boulder. Cursed.

Burrowing into the waist-deep grass, she kept low and crawled forward. Faster. Pushed harder. Needed as much distance as possible.

Shots pinged on the rocks.

J.T. scrambled alongside her.

He was breathing hard.

They had to stay close to the ground until they reached the next row of warehouses. Even though she was relatively certain they were out of range at this point, she wasn't taking any risks. And she wasn't slowing down.

J.T. had to keep up.

The splat of a bullet hitting the ground next to Eve had her rolling left. Maybe they weren't completely out of range.

She bumped J.T. He grunted.

His injured arm. Dammit. She could apologize later.

Half a dozen more yards.

Almost in the clear.

As she reached the cover of the alley between the first two warehouses she tensed.

Silence.

No pings or splats.

She glanced back at the dock. Deserted.

Time to run.

Her car was parked another block down.

Pushing to her feet, she sprinted forward. The wet bag dragged at her shoulder. She ignored it.

By the time she reached the lot where her car was parked, she had dug the keys from her pocket and hit the fob. Six seconds later she was behind the wheel. She hit the ignition as J.T. collapsed into the passenger seat. Tires squealed as she spun out of the slot.

"What the hell did you do to me?"

From the corner of her eye she watched him shake his head in an attempt to clear it.

He would be pissed when she told him about the tranquilizer.

She'd needed him cooperative until she formulated a plan. A drug-induced state of unconsciousness had been the fastest and most efficient method to ensure his continued solidarity.

"I can't really talk right now." Eve weaved into the right lane as the street widened to four lanes. What she needed was traffic. It was Saturday night—shouldn't be that difficult to find as soon as they were out of the old warehouse district.

A glance in the rearview mirror warned that their unwanted company had caught up.

Sensing her tension, J.T. turned to peer over his left shoulder.

"I hope you have a plan B."

She shot him a look. "There's always plan G." Then she pulled the Glock out of her waistband.

Cutting the steering wheel left, she slid between two vehicles. Another veer to the right and she'd put several cars between hers and the enemy.

She was betting they wouldn't pull out the firepower in the open like this, but a girl could never be too sure when it came to an unknown enemy.

Deep blending was the way to go.

Two traffic lights ahead the marquee of a movie theater provided exactly the opportunity she was looking for.

The digital numbers on the dash indicated it was just past midnight. Perfect timing. The late movie would be purging its audience into the crowd of teenagers who liked hanging out in the parking lot.

She took a hard right onto the property that sported a twelve-screen theater, numerous fast-food hot spots and a chain superstore. Speeding across the lot, she selected a lane of parking slots. Pulling in as close to the theater entrance as possible, she shut off the engine and reached for her door.

"Let's go."

Thankfully he didn't argue.

Rounding the hood of her car, she shoved the Glock into her bag, then wrapped her arm around J.T.'s and merged into the crowd.

With her free hand she finger-combed her long hair. It was soaked, as were her clothes. The kids she bumped into noticed, gave her death-ray glares.

They just didn't know.

As she and J.T. moved in closer to the building, she grabbed a baseball cap from an innocent bystander. The crowd made it easy. The kid who owned the cap had made it even easier by stuffing the cap bill-first into his waistband at the small of his back.

Pushing through the loitering crowd, she made her way to the side of the building next to the main entrance. She pushed J.T. against the wall and dropped her bag to the ground. Peeled off her tee and let it fall.

His gaze instantly zeroed in on her breasts, where the cami she wore had glued to her skin like an extra layer. A zing of desire shot through her veins.

Not the time.

With a flick of her wrist she twisted her hair up and clamped the cap atop the blond mass.

"They're coming," J.T. muttered as he gazed at some point beyond her.

"Yeah, I know." She planted her palms against the wall on either side of him and leaned in. "Keep your eyes open. Let me know when they're inside."

Then she planted her lips on his.

* * * * *

Will J.T. and Eve be caught in the moment?
Or will Eve get the chance to reveal
all of her secrets?
Find out in
THE BRIDE'S SECRETS
by Debra Webb
Available August 2009
from Harlequin Intrigue®

We'll be spotlighting a different series every month
throughout 2009 to celebrate our 60th anniversary.

LOOK FOR
HARLEQUIN INTRIGUE®
IN AUGUST!

To commemorate the event, Harlequin Intrigue® is thrilled
to invite you to the wedding of the Colby Agency's
J.T. Baxley and his bride, Eve Mattson.

Look for *Colby Agency: Elite Reconnaissance*

THE BRIDE'S SECRETS
BY DEBRA WEBB

Available August 2009

www.eHarlequin.com

REQUEST YOUR FREE BOOKS!

2 FREE NOVELS PLUS 2 FREE GIFTS!

Silhouette® Romantic SUSPENSE

Sparked by Danger, Fueled by Passion!

SRS09R

You're invited to join our Tell Harlequin Reader Panel!

By joining our new reader panel you will:

- Receive Harlequin® books—they are FREE and yours to keep with no obligation to purchase anything!
- Participate in fun online surveys
- Exchange opinions and ideas with women just like you
- Have a say in our new book ideas and help us publish the best in women's fiction

In addition, you will have a chance to win great prizes and receive special gifts!
See Web site for details. Some conditions apply.
Space is limited.

To join, visit us at
www.TellHarlequin.com.

In 2009 Harlequin celebrates
60 years of pure reading pleasure!

We're marking this occasion by offering
16 **FREE** full books to download and read.

Visit
www.HarlequinCelebrates.com
to choose from a variety of
great romance stories
that are absolutely **FREE!**

(Total approximate retail value of $60)

We invite you to visit and share the Web site
with your friends, family
and anyone who enjoys reading.

Silhouette®

Romantic

SUSPENSE

COMING NEXT MONTH

Available July 28, 2009

#1571 CAVANAUGH PRIDE—Marie Ferrarella
Cavanaugh Justice
When detective Julianne White Bear is sent from another town to
help hunt a serial killer, she brings with her a secret motive. Detective
Frank McIntyre has his hands full heading the task force, but he can't
deny his attraction toward Julianne—and the feeling is mutual. They're
determined to put romance on hold until justice is served, but it isn't
always that easy….

#1572 HER 24-HOUR PROTECTOR—Loreth Anne White
Love in 60 Seconds
FBI agent Lex Duncan and casino heiress Jenna Rothchild play each other
from the moment they meet. Even as the heat between the two sizzles
hotter than the Las Vegas desert, danger intensifies around them. Suddenly
Lex becomes the one man who can rescue the sexy young heiress…in
more ways than one.

#1573 HIS PERSONAL MISSION—Justine Davis
Redstone, Incorporated
Ryan Barton's teenage sister is missing, and his only hope to find her is
Sasha Tereschenko—the woman he'd loved and lost two years ago. Family
is everything to Sasha, who leaps into action. While the two track down the
predator possibly holding Ryan's sister, their former attraction arises again,
and their lives—and hearts—are put at risk.

#1574 SILENT WATCH—Elle Kennedy
Samantha Dawson has been in hiding since the night of her brutal attack.
Now, living in isolation under a new identity, she is surprised to find a sexy
FBI agent on her doorstep. Blake Corwin promises to protect Samantha in
exchange for her help with her attacker's latest victim. But the last thing he
expected was to fall for Sam, and when she again becomes a target, Blake
will do anything to save her.

SRSCNMBPA0709